The HarperCollins Book of New Indian Fiction

CONTEMPORARY WRITING IN ENGLISH

Edited by
Khushwant Singh

HarperCollins *Publishers* India
a joint venture with

New Delhi

HarperCollins *Publishers* India
a joint venture with
The India Today Group

First published in India in 2005 by
HarperCollins *Publishers* India

Third impression 2006

Copyright © Individual authors 2005

Each contributor asserts the right to be identified
as the author of his or her work.

Encounters with the Kodambakkam Hyena by Vivek Narayanan
was first published in *Agni* 61. Unfaithful Servants by Manjula Padmanabhan
was first published in *Hot Death, Cold Soup* (Kali for Women, 1996).

HarperCollins *Publishers*
1A Hamilton House, Connaught Place, New Delhi 110001, India
77-85 Fulham Palace Road, London W6 8JB, United Kingdom
Hazelton Lanes, 55 Avenue Road, Suite 2900, Toronto, Ontario M5R 3L2
and 1995 Markham Road, Scarborough, Ontario M1B 5M8, Canada
25 Ryde Road, Pymble, Sydney, NSW 2073, Australia
31 View Road, Glenfield, Auckland 10, New Zealand
10 East 53rd Street, New York NY 10022, USA

Typeset in 11/14 Simoncini Garamond
Atelier Typecraft

Printed and bound at
Thomson Press (India) Ltd.

Contents

Introduction

It gives me great pleasure to invite you to a feast of Indian fiction in its dainty, delectable and easily digestible form – a collection of the best short stories published in recent years. We may not yet have produced great novelists of the stature of Tolstoy, Mann, Scott or Dickens, nor playwrights of the calibre of Shakespeare, Goethe or George Bernard Shaw, but we have a rich heritage of poetry and short story writing. Here I am only concerned with short stories.

India has a long-standing oral tradition of narrating stories to audiences large and small. Traditionally, the oral form required them to be concise with a clear beginning, a build-up and a punch line in the end: clarity was paramount. That has continued to the present times. On the other hand, when you look at European or American short stories, you will often find their narratives smothered over with unnecessary digression, and many leave the reader hanging with an inconclusive conclusion.

The impact of Western literature, however, is clearly visible in contemporary Indian writing. Gone are detailed descriptions of the environment, diffuse moralizing and purple passages crammed with clichés, which were much in vogue till Independence. As in the West, so in India, short stories today are less parabolic, writers preferring to drive their points home in oblique, understated ways. They are no longer as inhibited in describing human relations, and are more and more concerned with problems facing a hidebound society in a fast changing world. In matters of form, too, modern Indian writers like their Western counterparts show a new willingness to experiment with the short-story structure.

The stories in this collection have been judiciously selected and represent the best of Indian writing around the world. Like Indian cuisine, they are as different as idli-sambar of the South is from tandoori chicken of the North, machher jhole from the East coast is from the pao-bhaaji of the West. And yet, they still retain a uniquely Indian flavour. I know in my gut you will enjoy reading them as much as I.

Khushwant Singh

If Brains Was Gas

Abraham Verghese

I TURNED THIRTEEN THAT WEEK. I ASSUMED THAT IT CAME with some new liberties, but no one had specifically said so, and I was too uncertain to ask. Still, the night after my birthday, Elmo and me made plans to go out. I washed and conditioned my hair when I got home from school, then dried it and combed it out. Usually I wore my hair in a French braid, but for that evening I left it loose. When I looked over my shoulder into the mirror, I liked the way my hair reached to my lower back.

I came out to the living room and sat on the edge of an armchair. My uncle, J.R., lay on the sofa where he had flopped down as soon as he came home from work, his jacket and boots still on, watching an *Andy Griffith* rerun. Mamaw – my grandmother – was sitting on her recliner, a cigarette sagging on her lips, the smoke above her head looking like the blurb of a cartoon, her hands busy with her puzzles. She glanced up at me and I knew she had me figured out. I had been about to ask Mamaw for permission to go out, but now I pretended to have come out of my bedroom to watch TV.

Mamaw let off a resonant fart and then settled back into the recliner, as if she were momentarily airborne.

'Sheba, Sheba,' Mamaw grumbled looking round her chair, but Sheba was in the kennel behind the house and could not be blamed for this one. J.R. and I exchanged glances; 'power farts' was what J.R. called them and he claimed they were the cause of the trailer being so loose on its foundation and the brick skirting starting to come loose. He wrinkled his nose, and pushed his front teeth halfway out his mouth. A laugh – though it sounded more like a hiccup – escaped me; I couldn't help myself.

Mamaw glared at me. 'Missy, I guess you done done all your homework? Or ain't you got none again?'

'Mamaw!' I said, knowing I had just blown my chance of going out, 'It was J.R.! He made me laugh. He pushed his teeth out!'

'Junior Hankins!' She put down her puzzle. 'Tell me, son, why did I pay an arm and a leg to have your jaw fixed so it wouldn't stick out like a lantern? For you to scare people half to death?'

J.R., not looking at her, raised off the sofa and leaned towards the TV as though something of the gravest importance had caught his attention: Bill Gatton of Gatton Ford-Hyundai-Mazda was dressed as an Arab and talking about a tent sale. Mamaw's eyes bored into J.R., but his own eyes became little slits as he studied the TV and tapped his temple with a thoughtful finger; he nodded as he listened to Arab Bill. I tensed up. Now I was in trouble with both of them.

'Thirty-one year old and act like a four year old,' was all Mamaw said. She turned back to her puzzle. J.R. kept his eyes on the TV. I had been holding my breath, and now I let it out. There was a step I felt I was missing, rules that no one had explained to me.

In a minute J.R. caught my eye and he did it again: his upper lip bulged, became pale as it stretched, then turned out to reveal the denture. It slid out like the head of a snail, it came to a rest, perched on his chin, pink, wet, and in a perpetual leer. When I was a baby, J.R. had stuck his teeth out at me and made me terrified of all men – this is what Mamaw told me – and I was two years old before I would go near my father who left soon after anyway. My mother (J.R.'s only sister) had disappeared soon after. Mamaw had raised me. J.R. had lived with us ever since I could remember. When he married Onesta, she joined us, which I always thought was one too many people to be living decently in a double-wide, but nobody had asked for my opinion.

'Missy,' J.R. said, heaving off the sofa, 'let's you and I go to Kmart. I need motor oil. Just run out.' He shook his key chain with the big-boobed mermaid. Jingle, Jingle, Jingle.

'She ain't going to Kmart or nowheres this time of night,' Mamaw said without looking up from her puzzle.

'Mamaw!' I said, sure that my date with Elmo was off, but hoping at least I would get to go with J.R.

'Ma,' J.R. said, 'we're going to Kmart, and she is plenty old enough to go out, and it's only seven-thirty, and Onesta ain't back from work yet, and supper ain't ready, so quit your whining, and think about dining. . .' He walked over behind her and bent over and kissed Mamaw noisily on the side of her face. When he raised up, he grimaced for my benefit, as if he had slammed into the stink wall behind her recliner.

My coat was on, my pocketbook was on my shoulder, and I was shining the doorknob with my sleeve, avoiding Mamaw's eyes, waiting for J.R., hoping Mamaw would say nothing to stop me.

I climbed into J.R.'s pickup and shut the door. 'Lock and load,' he said, just as the engine came to life. With one fluid, practised motion – I had never seen anyone else do this – J.R. flipped the heater on defrost, the fan on high, the radio on WJHW 104 FM, the headlights on high-beam, the parking brake off, the gear in reverse, pushed the cigarette lighter in, let the clutch out, and it seemed we were rolling before the 351 big block completed its first cycle. J.R. looked at me while he did all this, to show me that he did this entirely by feel and because he knew I appreciated this sort of talent. Elmo couldn't do nothing like that.

Sitting Big-Foot high in that cab, the night dark around us, the unlit gravel road crunching beneath our wheels, only the instrument lights glowing, I felt we were in the cockpit of our private plane, off on a secret mission. Only J.R. could make me feel this way. With his short beard growing high on his cheekbones, his close-set blue eyes that always made it seem as if he could see right through me, and the brown hair parted in the middle and longish like Jesus Christ, I thought he was the handsomest and sexiest man I knew. Kind of like the Alabama lead singer, though J.R. had done that look first. It was strange how I could be with Elmo, him smelling of hot water and soap, the Pinto giving off Pine Sol fumes, ten dollars in Elmo's pocket to burn, but never feel as good as I did with J.R.

At the first traffic light within the city limits, J.R. pulled up next to an old couple in a blue sedan and yelled through closed windows, 'Hey stupid!' and then stared straight ahead. The old man, thinking he heard something, looked up at us. J.R. turned to the old man as if to say 'What in the hell are you looking at?' The old man looked away. I wished I had peed before we left the house.

We pulled into Kmart and parked in a 'Handicapped' spot. A lady with giant curlers under her scarf and a shopping cart half-full of Alpo and paper towels scowled at us. J.R. put on a limp and let one hand curl up in front of his chest, spastic-like, and stumbled in her direction. She muttered and her little steps got faster and faster as she tried to skirt J.R. When J.R. stepped on the rubber mat and the door swung open, he was miraculously healed. His back straightened, his arm unfolded, his chin was held high, and he strode in as if he were Stonewall Jackson in Levi's, boots and black bomber jacket. And he knew I was behind him, watching.

We walked the aisles; I looked at the shelves while J.R. looked at the women. The place was full and Christmas music was still playing. The customers seemed relaxed and happy, while the store clerks looked harried. J.R. asked a brunette with a 'Let Me Help You' button whether condoms were sold in the hardware section. She gobbled and her eyes got goldfish big before she fled. 'Happy New Year,' J.R. called after her.

My heart was racing. Was it just coincidence that he asked about condoms? I started to check my purse, and then snapped it shut when I remembered the cameras above. They might think I was shoplifting. The speaker above my head blared 'Attention Kmart Shoppers' and J.R. stopped in mid-step and yelled: 'Yo!'

In Household Furnishings, J.R. sneezed his 'accshit' sneeze. People stared around aisles and between shelves. J.R. sneezed again, a double sneeze: 'accshit, aaaacshit,' leaving no doubts. He pushed his teeth out at an old lady who seemed hypnotized by him. I stood there. I knew people looked at me and thought I was J.R.'s girl. There was nothing I could do about that, and besides, it made me feel good. I wondered if J.R. felt the same way.

In the parking lot we ran into a guy J.R. knew. J.R. was fixing to buy dope. The guy's hair was extra long and he pushed it behind his ears, first one side then the other. His fingers had gnawed-down nails with clear polish on them and he had letters tattooed in the webs between his fingers. I studied his face to see if he felt stupid about any of this. I heard J.R. say, 'Don't worry about her. She's fine.'

We went to the guy's car and drove to the far end of the parking lot near the dumpster. He and J.R. lit up a fat joint and passed it back and forth, ignoring me. I sat in the back seat, looking out the side window, trying to breathe in as much of the car air as I could without drawing attention to myself. When they were ready to leave the car, I stepped out and almost fell on my face, grabbing the door. Back in the pickup, J.R. said, 'You high, squirt? I seen you trying to suck up all the air in the car.'

I shook my head, trying to look bored, but I was smiling and could not control it. I closed my eyes and leaned my head to one side. This was my test to see if I was high: if I was, my head would feel like a large boulder rolling down the side of a mountain. It felt that way now in J.R.'s pickup.

Elmo pulled in to Kmart just as we were pulling out. I made J.R. stop and roll down the window. I leaned over J.R. to hear Elmo. Elmo stuck his head out and twisted it up to talk to me. He had gone to my house looking for me, he said.

'I'm with J.R. tonight,' I replied, leaning against J.R., squishing him.

'So?' Elmo said. But his voice lost confidence. 'He's your uncle, right?'

'Damn!' J.R. said to Elmo, 'you really *should* go to college. Missy, he is *not* as dumb as he looks.' Traffic was backing up behind Elmo. A car honked and even though it was dark, I knew Elmo's face was turning beet-red. We pulled away.

'*If brains was gas,*' J.R. began, and I joined in, '*Elmo wouldn't have enough to prime a piss-ant's go-cart around a Cheerio.*' When we reached 'Cheerio' we were both rolling with laughter. I felt sorry for Elmo but I couldn't stop laughing.

Everyone in passing cars knew we were stoned. They were looking at us. Everyone knew. I was glad we were heading home.

J.R. looked down at a couple in a Corvette next to us at a traffic light. 'Holy mackerel, Missy,' he said, 'look at the cock-box on that young'un.' I didn't get a good look at the woman, just an impression of long legs and lipstick. 'Fuck her, buddy. I did,' J.R. shouted.

'What's a cock-box, J.R.?' I asked for no reason, thinking of how Elmo squirmed when I had wanted to study his hard-on. Elmo hadn't minded if I touched it, but he didn't want me to *look*.

'You *know* damn well what a cock-box is, squirt. Get fresh with me and I'll tell Mamaw all about you smoking dope and fumbling with Elmo in the burley shed.'

I felt my face turn red. J.R. laughed his 'Hee-Haw' laugh and said 'Fumblefumblefumblefumble', his lips a'splutter. I slapped at him. He can read my mind, I thought. The lollipop condom, floating in its juices and burning a hole in my pocketbook – he knows. Since I got the condom, I hadn't been with Elmo. Mamaw, and then J.R., had seen to it.

'I *control* Elmo,' I said to J.R. for no particular reason. 'That's what I like about him. *I control him.*'

J.R. looked at me strangely. 'Control this,' he said to me, sticking his middle finger in the air. I tried to break his finger, but my laughter made me a poor enforcer.

'You know something, squirt,' J.R. said in the pickup, as we rode back, stoned, from our Kmart, motor oil mission, 'I have found my *true* love. I have found the person who can satisfy me sexually, spiritually, and in every other way.'

'Yeah, I like Onesta too,' I said, lying through my teeth.

'Hell with Onesta. I don't mean Onesta.'

Does he mean me? My mind worked like slow treacle and no words came out. I felt tingly all over. My face was burning. I knew in the last year I had blossomed. My tits in profile were every bit as good as Cher's. And J.R. has seen me once when I had put on make up and heels when Mamaw was out shopping, and he had given me a wolf whistle. I didn't have slut eyes like Daisy Nunley, I didn't have knockers like Juanita Clayber, I didn't have a brother who pimped for me like Wanda Pearson. But I guess I had *something*, I knew that, and it was a good feeling. Mamaw knew it too and it made Mamaw extra surly and made her keep close tabs on me, and warn me about 'turning out like your dang-fool mother'.

'I don't know why I am telling you this, squirt,' J.R. continued, 'but I sure as hell don't mean Onesta.'

My stomach tightened. I felt like I had been in a car like this before and some other man said these same words. I looked around at the field whizzing by. I told myself: *I must remember this moment clearly.* I focused on a field on my side of the car, but the field had no boundary and as we drove by it went on forever.

'Me?' I blurted out. 'Do you mean me?'

J.R. laughed for a long time. He looked at me with admiration, as if he didn't know I could be so funny. A little girl inside me began to weep, even though I knew I should be relieved.

'Someone else, squirt. Not you. The love of my life. The reason for my living,' he said.

Did this mean J.R. would leave home I wondered. The thought of being alone with Mamaw – without J.R. or Onesta – crossed my mind and was painful. I thought of Onesta, Onesta from Oneida, raven-haired Onesta, pretty Onesta, dumb-as-a-coal-bucket Onesta. Yet, J.R. had always acted like he knew what he wanted from Onesta. And what she was – pretty and dumb – was exactly what he had wanted.

I found myself speaking: 'What the hell do you get married for in the first place? If you're just going to. . .' I was surprised at the half-sob in my voice. I turned away so he couldn't see my face.

J.R. gave this careful consideration. 'When I met Onesta, "*This is it*," I said. "This is it." So I got married.'

'Well you were dumb as shit for not knowing better.' The look of surprise on J.R.'s face reminded me of Elmo's face in the parking lot. '*This is it*, you said?' I continued, taunting J.R. '*This is it*? So what the hell happened? What happened to, *This is it*?' A part of me felt as if I were Onesta.

'Things happen,' I heard J.R. say. 'That feeling you have when you marry someone, when you love someone. . .it's great for a while, but it doesn't last. I met someone else now, Missy. She gives me that feeling again. It feels so good, squirt. I can't control it.'

'Same thing can happen again, J.R.,' I said softly.

He didn't say anything for a while. We were into fog again and he slowed the pickup. He lit up a fat roach that had been in his pocket and took in a deep drag. His eyes bugged out. 'Hell, *I* know that,' he said between his teeth, holding the smoke in. I snatched the roach from him. The pickup swerved as he tried to get it back. I leaned against my door, out of his reach, my feet raised, ready to kick him in the face. He backed off. I took deep leisurely drags, holding them in as long as I could.

'You're something else, Missy,' he said. 'Now, give that back. . .'

'Fuck you, Uncle,' I said. 'Fuck you, you big dummy. You can be so. . .funny, so. . .brave. But you're a *stupid shit* on top of that.'

I saw him flinch. He got serious, his eyes mournful, and I sat up and was just about to say I was sorry when he stuck his teeth out. I threw a punch at him, but he slipped it and it buried itself in the shoulder part of his jacket. He held his fist out, ready to bust me if I tried to hit him again. He was bobbing on the seat now, like Ali, jiggling his eyebrows up and down, a big grin on his face, stealing glances at the road, waiting for me to punch. 'The greatest of *all* time!' he said. I was still glad I didn't ride with Elmo.

When we came down our driveway it was almost eight o'clock. A car without lights came roaring out of the driveway and took off up the hill. I looked back and could see it was a Chevy hardtop.

'Who the fuck. . .' I said.

I didn't recognize it, but J.R. seemed to and was subdued. I could see that the car had stopped near the main road and now it waited, the engine running. Onesta's car was in the yard. J.R. sat in the pickup for a while and I waited with him. Something told me not to open my mouth.

J.R. entered the trailer through the kitchen door and I followed. Mamaw and Onesta were at the kitchen table, facing each other, smoking. Onesta's eyes were red. Mamaw had her bottle of Jack Daniel's on the table and was sucking on ice chips at the bottom of her glass. She looked mad. Maybe she had found out about the condom. Maybe Elmo came back and spilled the beans. Maybe the pickup truck was bugged. Maybe that car was the FBI and we were going to the slammer.

When Mamaw opened her mouth I thought she would ask me why my eyes were red. But she was looking right through me at J.R.

'It's about time you brought the young'un home,' Mamaw said softly.

'Missy, sweetheart, would you go to your room?' Onesta said, not looking at me, but staring at the table.

'What are you, her mother?' J.R. asked. His voice sounded funny.

Mamaw hissed: 'What are you, her father?'

'Could be,' said J.R., looking at Onesta.

Mamaw reached up and slapped J.R. across the cheek. The anger in her eyes was like nothing I had ever seen. My body felt heavy; I could not move.

'You tell Mamaw about your girl friend?' asked Onesta in a quiet, restrained voice.

'*You* tell her, Onesta,' he replied, glancing at the door that led to the living room.

'You tell Mamaw how she's married?'

'She ain't. . .married,' said J.R., a quaver in his voice that gave away his lie. The second hand of the kitchen clock was the loudest sound in the room. We all looked at him. I thought to myself: this is not real, this is not happening. But for the first time since we walked in, it dawned on me that this might have nothing to do with me.

Mamaw grasped J.R.'s shirt, almost fondling it, and slowly pulled him down so his face was inches from hers. She whispered, 'Read my lips, dummy. *She* is married. *You* are married. *Her goddamn husband is in the living room waiting to talk to you.*'

'She ain't married,' J.R. said. His voice has cracks in it.

The swinging door from the living room opened and a man I had never seen before walked in. I was sure he would have a gun in his hand. I wanted to pee in my pants.

He was squat and carried himself very upright so as not to waste inches. He was wearing a cream shirt, jeans and black loafers with white socks. He had red hair that was pulled from behind one ear in a sweeping arc to cover his baldness.

'Are you J.R.?' the man asked, pushing his glasses back on his nose. His teeth were even, with spaces between them. They were clearly his own teeth. His eyes were blue and clear.

I stepped away from J.R.

J.R. stepped behind Mamaw.

Mamaw sighed, her head bent over the table, and then she ground out her cigarette. J.R. looked around the kitchen – as though seeing it for the first time – and his Adam's apple bounced like a yo-yo. Mamaw poured a big dollop of Jack.

'I am Katherine's husband,' the man said.

J.R. seemed about to say something, his hands moved, but no words came out.

'Katherine done told me all about you and her,' the man said. 'She asked for my forgiveness and I've given it. She done confessed in front of the whole church. God has forgiven her. She confesses of her own free will.'

J.R. tried to look at the man while he spoke but could not hold his gaze.

The man continued, his voice rising in pitch, but very clear. 'I done forgiven you, too. I don't appreciate what you done to my family but I've forgiven you. I sure hope your wife can do the same.'

Onesta began to cry. J.R. tried to glare her down but she was not looking at him, and besides this was not the time for it.

'I will ask that you stay clear of *my* wife. I don't want to see you anywhere around her,' the man said.

J.R. looked at the wall behind the man's head. The man turned to go out through the swinging door. He stopped and bowed his head as though about to add something, and then, thinking the better of it, left. We heard the Chevy pull into the driveway and then drive out.

No one spoke in the kitchen.

J.R. took a deep breath as if to compose himself, to ready his explanation.

Onesta took a long sip from Mamaw's glass. Neither Mamaw nor Onesta would look at J.R. He looked at me over their bowed heads. He tried to get the mischief back into his eyes but they appeared shallow and shifty. He tried to smile, but his cheeks were quivering and the smile threatened to degenerate into a sob.

I waited.

J.R.'s eyes pleaded with me.

As if with a will of its own, his denture came pushing out at me – an offering. Under his sad eyes, he gummed the denture. It glistened with saliva. His upper lip was flabby and sunken. It was pathetic, like an old man's nakedness.

Then, in what I think now was the cruellest moment of my life, I yelled at him: 'You big dummy!'

Mamaw and Onesta looked up surprised at my outburst, but I continued, 'You big dummy! If brains was gas. . .you, you. . .'

I walked out. My eyes were blurry and my feet slipped on the gravel road. I took deep breaths. I took the condom from my purse and ripped its cover off with my teeth. I chewed the condom, tasting the oily lubricant, hearing it squeak as I ground it to a pulp. I felt a calmness, a sense of who I was, a sense of completely inhabiting my body. It was like nothing I had ever experienced.

Diablo Baby

Githa Hariharan

WHICH ONE OF YOU IS MY FATHER?

I know what you, with the twitching lips, and you, and you – with the knotting eyebrows and bulging notebook – will say. The obvious thing. Ask your mother.

I have. She speaks to me (and sings to me and dances for me) just as a mother should. And I, Diablo Baby, talk to her. I never gooed and gaaed and gurgled like other mothers' babies. Why pretend to be ordinary when you are not?

But when I ask her the big question, all she can do is show me a tattered rag of a sari. It is bleached cotton, so old, frayed and grimy that it could be a strip of dry bark curling at the edges. But the picture on it glistens; white chalk flesh, yellow and red hibiscus of vegetable dye. There is a body in the picture, a body that has trapped the glint of silver in its bulges and ripples and folds. A piece of bloated moon that sits on a carpet of succulent forest flowers, on a sheet of smooth, fiery blood.

I have looked at this image many times. In it my reflection holds still. (When I look at myself in the stream, the water trembles, afraid of my steady gaze, my horns, my tattoos.)

My mother made the picture. She also made me. She thinks she had some help there, though she knows no names to name. When I ask her, Where is my father, she replies, In my head.

Then you came, she says, so we don't need him any more. And we have the picture, don't we? And the story in the picture?

So if I want a father, I must mine a story as strange and raggedy as my mother. A story with a forest girl, a temple, a church, a baby. And a blue-white, horned, phantom lover.

On the edge of the forest was a village and in the heart of the village were two buildings, one on the right side of the dusty street, one on the left. The buildings could have been brothers, so alike were their mortared, whitewashed walls. But like many brothers, their heads were somewhat different. The building to the right, a temple, had a brick pyramid for a head. A tapering triangle of a gopuram sat like a stiff hat pulled down over its face. At the tip of this hat, a solitary red flag waved in the breeze. A piece of the flag was cut out of its right side so that what remained was a trembling, open mouth.

The building to the left, a church, had a more modest, flat head. But a huge bell filled up the balcony that jutted out of its forehead. Even bigger and more impressive was the cross crowning the roof. The cross was painted a dazzling white that sucked in the sunlight and threw a halo round itself.

*

Every morning at daybreak, a girl in a torn, dirty sari carrying a basket and a broom made her way to the temple. As usual there was a big brass tray waiting for her on the step nearest the open front door. She put down her broom and uncovered the basket that was covered with a piece of damp cloth. She emptied the basketful of blazing red and pink and orange hibiscus onto the brass plate. Then she picked up the broom and went round to the backyard where yesterday's flowers lay in a limp and fleshy pile along with everything else that had been swept out of the temple. She filled up the basket with this rubbish, sorting it out first to see what was there. Anything edible she pulled out and slipped into the little bundle tied to the end of her sari.

The temple-priest called out to her as he did every morning. Hey Sukhi, he said. The flowers are really fresh this morning. I don't know where you manage to find them. Do you want some pieces of coconut?

Sukhi nodded and he threw a large handful in her direction. She picked up the pieces and sat on her haunches, chewing.

He lingered at the back door while she ate. He was bald, with a tuft of hair at the back of his head. He was always bare-chested, and the jungle of dark hair on his chest made him look like a tame bear.

He frowned at the broom lying by her.

Still working for the foreign devil? he asked. Why do you go to the white man's temple?

Sukhi stopped chewing and considered this with puzzlement. Who is a devil? she asked. And why is he white?

He sniggered and threw her a few more pieces of coconut. You'll find out soon enough, he said, looking at her knowingly. You keep sweeping that church day after day and you'll meet the devil all right. A white devil with a blazing cross on his heart. Grey eyes shining out of his chalk face like a hungry cat.

Sukhi picked up her broom and basket. You stop working there if you know what's good for you, he called after her.

Sukhi swept the church with her broom; her basket was now filled to the brim with junk from both temple and church. Then she dusted and polished the silver cup at the altar.

The church-priest gave her a coin. He also gave her something to eat. She liked sitting in the church's backyard, chewing and thinking her own thoughts. But neither the temple-priest nor the church-priest could leave her alone. Neither could do without her, so lovely and fresh were the flowers she brought every morning, and so well did she sweep and dust and polish.

Now the church-priest began his usual sermon as she ate. Still taking flowers to that temple? he asked, eyeing the wilted flowers in her basket.

My child, he said, his voice growing rich and sonorous. Come home to this church and be saved. Remember what I have told you. The devil is always watching you from where he sits burning in hell. He waits, the devious snake, to open his mouth and strike. He is horned; he is lecherous. When he sees the bare breasts under your sari, when he finds your untouched soul, do you think he will let you go?

Ah, the devil again, thought Sukhi, and she listened carefully. Though the temple-priest and the church-priest can't bear each other, they have this mysterious devil in common.

Her head was full of the devil as she made her way back into the forest. The forest was still, in a deep, stupefied sleep. In fact, the forest that afternoon was a fit place for the devil, if he really liked fire as much as the priests said he did. She could feel the relentless fire on her head and back and feet as she made her way, a single thought throbbing in her head, never pausing till she reached the pool. The watering hole was deserted except for a few thirsty birds that took wing as she neared the water.

She was hot, so hot. She pulled the filthy sari off her body and went naked into the water. The world outside her closed eyes was a furious blur of orange.

She thought she felt something cool slither up her leg. It could have been a water snake, but she did not move. Instead she heard herself whispering playfully, teasingly, Devil, are you here? Are you watching me?

She floated. She must have floated for hours, or floated into sleep, or into a dream. In this place where she had drifted, a girl like a lost and empty boat looking for its moorings, the fiery world waiting outside her eyelids had vanished. The heat had dissolved, so had the priests and her hungry sunburnt body in the muddy forest pool. The cool-tongued intruder making his way up her leg lived in this place where there was no thirst, no drudge of filling the belly. The fire on her skin was being put out. The anger and bewilderment in her heart were dying. And at the very last moment, just before the coolness slipped out of her and left her, she saw, though her eyes were still shut, an image she could capture again in meticulous, three-dimensional detail. She need never be alone again. She saw a baby plump with her desire, sharp-horned, self-possessed. On his body he flaunted all the caste marks of his paternity, or the lack of it.

Encounters with
the Kodambakkam Hyena

Vivek Narayanan

V. P. SUNDERARAJAN AND HIS WIFE PADMINI HAD TAKEN TO rising as late as 7.30 a.m. They gulped down their coffee and sometimes went for a walk. After that, she ground grams while Sunderarajan sulked with the radio on 'Joke Hour', vacantly glazing his eyes over the newspaper. What is it now, he thought, when he heard the buzz of the bell. Retired life is boring, everybody knows, but is it possible for something so boring to be also exhausting? No time even for coffee, before bloody the doorbell. He hawked, spat his mouth out into the sink, and went to the door.

It was one of Sunderarajan's closest juniors from the old branch. Behind him stood a small, very jumpy looking man with a neat caterpillar of a moustache, who was wearing a pair of stonewashed jeans and a genuine Lacoste T-shirt with the collar turned up.

'Pandiarajan!' Sunderarajan said to his junior, muffling his irony. 'Just in time. Would you like some degree coffee?'

'Saar, lovely to see you. No, half-cup, thank you saar. This is my maternal aunt's son, saar.'

The jumpy man stepped up, head slightly bowed, and introduced himself in Tamil: 'Pu. Zha. Sunderarajan is the name. What are your initials, sir? What is your phone number?'

'They have called me Indian Bank Sunderarajan,' No. 1 replied shyly. He noted to himself that Sunderarajan No. 2 appeared to be fair, forties, and foreign returned – what of his daughter, studying engineering at Manipal? – no, too old – and motioned the two early visitors to their seats. No. 2 was Sunderarajan's junior by some twenty years and the smell of vibhuti mixed with a strong French aftershave emanated from him. At the moment, he also looked to be puzzled.

'No, no, sir – your initials, I mean,' he was saying in English. 'For instance, I am Pee Zed Sunderarajan.'

Our No. 1 was a little irked because the new visitor had not even raised a polite eyebrow to the Indian Bank name; but he replied proudly, 'V.P. Sunderarajan, Velpadi Pattabhirama Sunderarajan.'

'Nice to meet you, V.P., sir.' P.Z. continued, with the tactful voice of a doctor. 'You are looking to see what will happen on the investment scene, sir?'

The purpose of the visit was becoming rapidly clear. Pandiarajan dabbled in astrology, and had long predicted a financial blossoming for V.P.; having prophesied it, he wanted more than anything to also be an agent of its fulfilment.

'You see, saar,' V.P. said, concerned to not look like a fool, 'it is the core fund which is being depleted and we are anticipating a use of spot funds for our daughter's marriage. After all, if she is matched with, or better still meets herself a gem of a boy, we would not want to look like penny-pinchers at the wedding.' V.P. leaned back, blinking.

'Sir,' P.Z. continued with a faint air of pity, 'government bonds, postal schemes and so on only protect you against inflation, sir, that is the problem.'

Pandiarajan said, 'He is offering 35 percent back, saar.'

This was the mid 1990s, when the banks themselves were offering up to 12.5 percent; V.P. quickly calculated in his mind that with 35 percent you could double your seed money in about two years. 'MNC stocks ahn?' he asked cautiously.

'Why MNC? I.T.-sexy? Look around, sir. This is not the India of yesteryear! We have finally come up.'

P.Z. and Pandiarajan then proceeded to inform V.P. that in the industrious city of Chennai, and the state as a whole, there were certain people who needed money loaned to them at exorbitant rates in a hurry – honest businessmen, some of them in films, and yes, even a dot com or two. 'People need loans to build things, the city's buildings are getting closer to the sky faster,' Pandiarajan said. 'Please sir, have some coffee, think it over for a day before responding. People like you and I with bright daughters may be in need of spot cash, saar.'

When, later, he thought back to that moment, V.P. was surprised to note that evil had made an appearance in his life so simply, and had belonged to the world of statistical stocks and interest rates. The men were not imposing. By the time puckering Padmini, hoping to make a quick getaway, arrived in the living room with coffee, the visitors were ready to leave.

Sunderarajan's wife was a tall, skinny, scraggly-haired woman with a throaty voice. She usually confessed to herself an innate distrust of most humanity but also took a more serious view of their financial mire. 'What is wrong with having cash?' she said. 'If we don't invest it, it'll slowly drain. Why don't we put in a small amount and see what happens?'

It was nearing bedtime; the prime-time TV serials were wishing their last jingling farewells. In the remarkably cool night (there had just been a surprising ten-minute rain) V.P. went to close the door to the narrow balcony. He paused on the floor and peered at his ankle, which was being pricked by something nearly invisible: the fine translucent thread of a miniature mosquito's legs, then the black-and-white fleck of its body. 'Alas, no amount of money will be enough to banish your people from ours,' he said to the mosquito. And, chuckling, 'We are blood relations.' But, just as he was getting up to close a window along the way, an unpleasant stream of dust and hot air hit him in the face, and he cursed, cancelling the karma earned with the insect: 'Ah bloody what condition that air is in! What blackguards they are, in cool weather!'

Why should he find the hot, purging blast from the rumbling backside of an air conditioner, from a neighbour's window directly opposite, more difficult to tolerate than a blood-sucking mosquito? Sunderarajan, who was interested in Universal Law, reasoned that this was because he could solve the former problem: by simply closing his window, and buying the same unit, or two, or even central air-conditioning if necessary, for *his* flat. If he had the money. The logic seemed unassailable: it was mankind's primary duty to fulfil its own flowering, and money was only the means and not the end of development.

When he reached a logical answer, Sunderarajan was a decisive man. Easing into bed, he said, 'Okay. You win. What amount do you think we should try out?'

'You always make it seem like I am the one who wants to spend,' Padmini replied, wounded. 'If you don't have specific numbers for me, let's wait and see what Pandiarajan says.'

To their irritation, Pandiarajan and his maternal aunt's son showed up the very next day, again in the midst of the retired bank officer's gargling. This time they brought some paper.

Pandiarajan had a printout, in an enthusiastic typeface, of planetary alignment diagrams – which demonstrated that for Sunderarajan's particular sign, a Maham-Moolam cusp, financial stability would return in approximately three to six months if the appropriate preparations were made; of course, this was all under rebellious Saturn, so there could be no absolute certainties. V.P. was unimpressed by Pandiarajan's technology, and was more interested in the second Sunderarajan's printout, which listed the names of all the people who were investing with him currently. Sunderarajan No. 2 used the fork of his long index and middle fingers to languidly underline the names on the list. 'Do you know? This man is actually a producer and soundman for films. And this man, a director. And, ah yes. Retired police commissioner, very good man.'

V.P. did not know the names on the list, but they had a ring of truth, or forgotten memory, about them. On the other hand, Padmini, who was a little disturbed by the odd picture that P.Z. cut in her living room – Jackie Shroff hairstyle and a large watch; that strong, straight, stone of a nose; those square, black, plastic cooling-glasses – admitted to some nervousness much later. Besides, she thought, who had ever heard of a name beginning with *zha*? She could only think of *Jean*, in Saddhananda Bharathi's translations of Victor Hugo!

'You are distrusting him for being a stylish, quirky fellow,' V.P said, holding his bedtime *Reader's Digest* to the light. 'Of course there are risks involved. This man knows what he is doing – by introduction only, mind you. And he will not have built his business in a day, madam.'

The next morning the two were under-slept, and more or less resigned to 'promoting their capital development'.

Pandiarajan was at the door just before lunch. 'The truth of the fact is, saar, he is a bigger fish in town than both of us put together; but luckily, he is a gentleman. I don't know about some of those fellows he lends to, though,' Pandiarajan said, slurping rasam off his palm. 'Anyway – I have seen him since young age, so I put in ten lakhs last year, and returns have been coming. But I think that will be too much for you, initially. Why don't you throw some two lakhs in, see what happens? If you don't get 35, you'll at least get 29-30. One thing I can say – he's certainly a brilliant man. I think he studied at either Oxford or Cambridge. You should hear him hold forth in English; he can quote long passages from Pope and Macaulay.'

'But,' Sunderarajan said, patting and rubbing Pandiarajan's back, 'He will be requiring cash, I suppose?'

'Cash is very much preferred, saar. I personally have seen his accounts and have no cause to worry.'

Poor Pandiarajan, his dark brow glistening with sweat, had suffered much greater difficulties than he, after his son had been born with Down's syndrome. And V.P. knew that his colleague was not an immoderate or corrupt man either.

As a bank officer, Sunderarajan had frequently overseen the large amounts of cash even petty businessmen brought in; but he still thrilled to carry such a sum when it was his own. It would not be much, in big denominations – two small red-brown paper packets, fitting in his front pockets if necessary. He would wrap them in a cloth, fit them neatly into a jewellery bag, and even on the bus he would be safe. All the other big-time investors, Pandiarajan informed him, had paid in cash; nevertheless, V.P. Sunderarajan was not a man to do things without paper work.

When he arrived in an autorickshaw at the gates of P.Z.'s apartment block, mildly perfumed, wearing a cyan safari suit, he was carrying only two hundred rupees in bills and, in a slim leather briefcase, a chequebook. A pleasant, very bulky security guard walked with him into the building, Nandini Mini-Village: the ugliest glitzy-shiny glass-filled shambles of a brand-new building that V.P. had ever cast eyes on! He could patently see the poor workmanship on the expensive building and the foolhardy contortions – soon likely to cause problems – that it had been put through, simply to fulfil a fusion of Vastu Shastra conditions and some ambitious architect's futuristic vision! Sunderarajan sighed deeply, mentally totalling the amount that might have been spent in excess. Some people are very wasteful when they are having money, he cautioned himself.

They passed the bright indoor swimming pool that pumped itself with gushing fresh water, when the building gently blinked – for two or three seconds – and flickered back to life, in time to the generator's rasping tremor. They took a lift that was large but slow; V.P. and the guard struggled to avoid each other's faces in its wall-to-wall mirror. Finally, the lobby of P.Z.'s floor opened out and they went to his big orange buzzer.

P.Z.'s wife, a very fair-skinned and beautiful woman in her late thirties, made-up, answered the door. 'We were just getting ready to go to the Cosmopolitan Club for a charity meeting,' she said, politely. Behind her, a milk-whistle persisted. 'But please come in.'

He heard P.Z.'s voice from around the corner. 'Meera, you carry on. The driver's there, isn't he? Mr Sunderarajan is here on business. Prior appointment. Please sir, come into my study.' The broker's voice had grown nasal, hoarse and slightly British.

'You're having a cold, saar?' V.P. said. He walked into the study, which was lined from floor to ceiling with wooden bookshelves – that were in turn filled with brown, bound volumes. Along one face stood a metallic blue almirah and a glass cabinet, with a computer and office seat stationed in between; the surrounding setup gave to the chair a throne-like presence.

P.Z. sat elsewhere, in a dark corner by the window, quickly putting down a glass that was in his hand. 'Shall I make you a drink?' he asked, without a trace of embarrassment. He was wearing a deep orange Lacoste shirt and what might have been the same pair of jeans. That man is always wearing Lacoste and jeans, V.P. wondered. Was it meant to be some kind of uniform?

V.P. said, 'Thank you saar. No alcohol for me. You carry on.'

Suddenly sounding much less British, but still hoarse, P.Z. yelped, 'No, no. If you are not taking sir, then I will also refrain.' He switched on a study light, motioned to a chair near him, and put on a pair of reading glasses. 'Tell me. How can I help?'

'I would prefer to write you an account payee cheque,' V.P. said in an indulgent, avuncular tone. 'Will you kindly provide me with your company's name?'

P.Z. whistled through bared clenched teeth. 'Sir, the company's name is Nandini Finance, after this building – you see, we are literally a cash cow, cash only, sir. Look here – ' he got up, went to the other side of the study and unlocked the almirah, which was far taller than he was.

Inside was a shoebox that contained neatly arranged rows of rubber-banded bill packets. P.Z. took out a packet from the box and began to scratch the bills down their sides with his thumbnail, making a *krrk-krrk-krrk* sound, separating them. 'This is how much I have made just today, sir. It was not hard to do. What's more, my debtors are the type to insist only on brand-new bills. There is no problem, no problem at all.' He put down the notes, flapped his spiky long hair upward with his palm, then motioned to V.P. to sit on the office chair and look at the screen.

'See. This I showed you, no? The list of people who have invested with us. But you can look at the amounts, too, if you wish, sir. You inspire an absolute trust in me.' P.Z. leaned over from the other side of the console and continued, chuckling darkly, 'I am Sunderarajan the second.' He contorted himself to squint at the several zeroes on the monitor with his client. For his small size, he appeared to have a remarkably strong and agile body. Skinny, gangly V.P. shifted uneasily in the office-chair-throne, underlining the names on the screen with the mouse pointer, partly to show that he was also familiar with computers. He felt trapped and short of breath. The acetate-like whiff of the newly printed notes on the desk, in the cool air-conditioned room, made him feel slightly nauseous. He closed his eyes and opened them again, meeting the glare of P.Z.'s spectacles.

'I can only give you a cheque, saar. But I understand my investment would be minor for you. Perhaps I will consider the matter for a few more weeks and call you if I still want to –'

'No, no, sir,' P.Z. half-barked, widening his grin and blowing more air through his teeth. He patted the wad of cash. 'Non-cash is inconvenient and time-consuming, that is all I am saying. Inconvenient. Very inconvenient. Shall I take this and call you after the cheque has been cleared? How did you come? Let me see – I shall call my wife and tell her to send back the driver. I'm sure he can leave you home on his way back to the Cosmopolitan Club. No problem, no mention.'

V.P. Sunderarajan refused the driver as a matter of principle, and was glad, even later, that he had done so. He felt proud to have stood his ground on the question of a cheque, a small assurance of security from the younger Sunderarajan, who had – perhaps by relying on less than legal means – many of the things he wished for in life. When he reached home to a tight-lipped Padmini, he did not feel triumphant, only tired.

According to his records, the first interest payment did arrive as a cheque forty-five days later, and the second payment a month after that, so the gradually rising digits of his bank statement becalmed our retired bank officer for a while. With Padmini's approval, he put another two lakhs into Nandini Finance, thereby sinking a little more than a third of their life savings into P.Z.'s venture. Their interest payment doubled as planned, until in the fourth month, when it returned mysteriously to its earlier level. V.P. rang up P.Z. to complain, and P.Z.'s wife answered. 'Don't worry, sir. There is just a temporary block in the pipeline. You will get the balance within eleven days. No Uncle, he is not in the house at the moment, but he has given this message not just for you, but for twenty-two other creditors also. Computer error.' She inhaled sharply. 'My husband will surely pay for this mistake. I hope he has learned his lesson.' Thirteen days later, a cheque for the balance of the interest arrived and Sunderarajan let out a dark – partly staged – sigh of relief. Meanwhile, his wife had developed some throat inflammation.

Over the next five months, almost like the city's rain, the interest came in dribs and drabs, and gradually petered out; and by that time, V.P. had also become drained of any energy he might have had to chase it down. Worse, it dawned on him that his insistence on writing cheques to a company would only make it harder for him to hold an individual accountable. He became, by turns, irritable, glum, then stoic. When, at the end of it all, the bank returned Nandini Finance's cheque a third time, he could only languorously mutter, setting aside the envelope, sitting down to scan the matrimonials for Vadagalai Brahmin bridegrooms: 'After all, what if my daughter meets some French fellow? She may be happy.' He had already decided that this episode was meant to be a punishment from the universe for his greed.

'How can we let him cheat us out of our money?' Padmini seethed. Her voice was cracking. 'He is expecting us to keep quiet. We must do something.'

Sunderarajan said, '*We* must do? You only make *me* do everything. Why don't you make a suggestion and implement it yourself? That man is a very strange bad-fellow, he can't get caught, you don't know anything.'

'But if he is a bad-fellow, we must simply get a lawyer.'

'We will have to give bribes to the lawyer, but he may have the judge in his pocket, you don't know.'

'If you know so much, why did you agree to this in the first place?'

Thus, though she was in pain, it was Padmini who had to invoke her inner Draupadi on the phone: 'Tell me Meera, I am asking you as a woman to a woman, have mercy, do you believe in truth? Do you believe in such a thing as truth? Does your husband?'

'Maami,' Meera said, sounding shocked, 'why are you straining your throat? Why don't you put Uncle on the phone?'

'Uncle is lying down.'

This was technically true. V.P. was lying on the bed and Padmini was sitting next to him. 'Maami!' Meera said. 'You don't know what I have to go through day after day. He doesn't tell me anything anymore.'

'You live in the same house, don't you? Why can I not talk to him myself? You tell him to call us back sometime today or we will just go to the police.'

Three hours later, just after 11 p.m., the phone rang, and she moodily scrambled for the receiver. At first she could only hear the sound of breathing. 'Hello, hello?' Then, a very strange but very human sound.

'Oooo-whup, oooo-whup!'

'Hello, hello?'

'Oooo-whup, oooowhup!'

'What nonsense!' Mrs Sunderarajan said, looking at the mouthpiece.

V.P. called out from the bathroom. 'Padmini, what is the problem?'

She put the instrument to her ear again and heard more raspy breathing, then something that sounded like a very soft growl. 'Daughter of mine, is that you?' she asked. The growl turned into more of a whimper. This frightened her, and a sharp pain flashed from her neck as if syringes were poking in it. The first call came again.

'Ooooo, Ooooo, Ooo-whep!'

'Wrong number,' she said. She was gently lowering the receiver towards its stand when she thought she heard a woman's voice jabbering from the earpiece. It was Meera Sunderarajan.

'Aunty, he is having a breakdown, that's why he's acting like this.'

Before Padmini could respond, P.Z.'s voice – she felt sure now that he had made the noises – came on again in English.

'Aunty? Hello Aunty-madam? I want to tell you something. I have thirty concubines, okay? Thirty. I can tell my wife to go to hell.'

'Mr Sunderarajan, I don't know what you are talking about, but we would like our money back. The interest does not matter.'

'No, madam, it is you who does not understand. I have at least thirty concubines. I take them from the front and then

I take them from the back. I have thirty concubines and I know every goonda in this town, from top to bottom! I'll have you shot! You don't know what I can do!'

In the background, Padmini could hear Meera saying, 'Aunty, please, he doesn't know what he is saying!'

'Shaddap!' P.Z. barked. Then, back into the receiver, 'Aunty? Madam? I will have you shot, okay? I will have you shot.' And he hung up the phone.

A busy tone came on. With the receiver still bleating in her hand, Padmini fell back to the bed, shaken. She imagined P.Z., with his confident eyes, pulling out a gun and shooting her. 'What is the matter, let me die,' she said, melodramatically testing the words in her mouth.

Rather belatedly, they learnt from a distraught and distracted Pandiarajan that, truth be told, P.Z. had been acting increasingly strange over the past few months: he had been seen spending long, late-night hours in the security booth of Nandini Mini-Village, smoking beedis with the guard, and the previous week, apparently, someone had seen him walking around on all fours in the lobby of the building.

V.P. Sunderarajan reacted to this news with scepticism. What if it was all an act, to frighten his creditors while the fellow filed for bankruptcy? On further enquiry, he found that, although P.Z. was reportedly seeing a psychiatrist, no further action had been taken. He continued to be a presence at the building society's meetings and at the Cosmopolitan Club, where he stayed his suave old self and had no 'episodes'. He was living happily in the lap of luxury, thanks to the money of his creditors, and he seemed to have no intention of parting with it. But to V.P.'s chagrin, Pandiarajan saw the matter differently.

'It is a terrible tragedy, saar. My aunt is saying she wants to commit suicide. He was such a brilliant boy and now this has happened to him.'

'But what about money? Does he not still have all our money? Is he not living off it?'

Pandiarajan looked taken aback for a second, then quickly hid his disappointment and switched to a suppliant tone. 'God willing, saar, he will get back on his feet soon and get the money back. But if not saar, I am so sorry, I promise I will give you the money out of my own pocket.'

'But we cannot take money from you!' Padmini said. 'What about your son?'

Indeed. Pandiarajan had no reply. The conversation reached an impasse.

Another week passed, and it slowly sunk in for Sunderarajan and his wife that their money might never come back. Padmini spoke vaguely of lawyers, made some enquiries, and half-heartedly flipped through the yellow pages, but V.P. laughed derisively at her suggestions, and pictured himself having to ritualistically appear for court date after court date. Technically, with his pension, it would still be possible for them to have almost the same standard of living; but their sense of defeat – *my final defeat*, thought V.P. – meshed with a deeper malaise.

Nearly a year had passed since they had first invested with Nandini Finance, and they had received only about 15 percent of their original sum back, as interest. Padmini took to her needlepoint and novels with an increasingly grim concentration; Sunderarajan slept for longer and longer in the summer. They had even begun to lose interest in finding a match for their daughter, who was now working in Mumbai and did not seem to want to visit or call. They hardly talked, to each other or to anyone else.

He now preferred to go on his grocery-shopping bicycle ride in the late afternoon and not the morning, a time of the day when all he could feel was anguish and dread. Early on one of these evenings, returning with milk, he was riding slowly back to his colony, clutching his bicycle's brakes. As usual, he rode past the large, glass-fronted, swank three-floor department store where he never shopped, and through the brief cool pocket of air that the building's powerful air-conditioning was actually projecting all the way to the road. He rode further, onto a side street, and noticed that, oddly, there suddenly appeared to be no young about; the streets seemed only full of people in their sixties and seventies, or even older: one was rising and falling on the flat street with the help of a cast-iron four-legged walking device; another, a very small woman in a bright blue sari, wizened to a wisp, dirty, was lost in herself and prayers between her forehead and fingers; and a third was wearing the banner of a sweat-bandana, strutting down the right side of the road with a defiantly vacant look, smoothing his white hair, engaged in celebrating his health, moving his arms about. There was a man who was likely a retired police officer, by his well-tended moustache, paunch, white shirt and khaki pants, carrying a big mobile phone and a brightly polished but old lathi; and there was a fat old woman with a purple face, grumbling about dollars to her smaller, rounder, very old mother. The sky darkened, and Sunderarajan's sense of hearing was heightened until he could hear a woman from a first floor window, on the telephone – 'No, no, you must come now, he's unwell' – and another, slim, hair thinning, carrying a folder, humming a Hindi song, wearing a dress. She tested the ground in front of her with a walking stick.

The streetlights, taxed by the late-closing factories, glowed reddish yellow at half-mast, and hump-like shadows appeared along the road. Sunderarajan heard the trumpets of trucks but none were to be seen. Barely three minutes from home, while he was skirting a ditch, his front tire knocked against a large building stone; he jumped off the bicycle and pushed it to the road, but in the process his hand slapped against the protective tape around the ditch, which in turn took with it a supporting wooden stake. He got up, after a moment, and determined to fix the stake back, peering into the ditch to see where it had gone. Immediately inside the ditch was what seemed to be a sleeping body, a child's, but it looked to Sunderarajan – from the rictus grin of its face, the teeth glowing – like a corpse. He looked up, and the road's edges seemed to be unevenly lined with bodies, all the way that he had come. With sudden clarity, he understood that all the people he had seen some few minutes ago on his ride had been P.Z.'s investors too; that they had died, that they had always been dead. He saw blurry numbers as if they were specks of dust in his eyes, rising and falling to an incalculable formula. He cried out, 'Celestial law, why have you punished me so?' as if to shout this could be a kind of protection.

A heavy hand clapped on his shoulder, and the vision cleared. 'What, saar, do you not have any common sense? Are you not an educated man? We must be careful when we are riding two-wheelers, at our age.' V.P. turned to find the man with the white shirt and khaki pants; he was about three inches taller, much broader, and was squinting. He now looked vaguely familiar, as if he were someone V.P. ought to know. A thought appeared in V.P.'s head: could this in fact be the retired police officer who had invested with P.Z. Sunderarajan? They began to walk down the dark road together, the man with the handlebar moustache kindly dragging the bent bicycle along by its handlebars and, strangely enough, it emerged that he *was* the very same retired police commissioner, one Mr Murugan.

'I had invested some money some three years ago,' Murugan said, 'and I had to go and recover it from him last year. I wanted to get him in jail also, but as you know the courts are taking their time, and the rascal is good at using his pull and paying off lawyers, even for the prosecution. So still he is having new victims! The younger fellows at the station are calling him the Kodambakkam Hyena now, because of his latest antics. It is all a pretence to scare people, but what can you do?' He paused and made a wistful *chups* sound with his lips. 'The problem, saar, is that we are not able to inform the public in a timely manner. And what about the rest of the people in his building? They are knowing but they are not doing anything. The police are simply happy to do a good deed or two, but most of the problems, we are not the persons to fix them.' Then, looking at V.P.'s sagging frame, he said, 'Why don't you come with me to the fellow's place and we'll see what we can do?'

V.P. had already gone to Nandini Mini-Village twice in the past month, with the hope of intercepting P.Z. The first time he had slowly circled its perimeter in an auto but had not told the driver to stop; something about the grotesqueness of the looming dark-pink construction itself had intervened. The second time, feeling stronger, he had insisted that the security guard let him in, and the large guard had told him – in a manner first stern, then soft, then stern again – that Mr P.Z. Sunderarajan and his wife had left for a temple tour in the Thanjavur district and would not be back for a week. V.P. had felt instinctively sure of P.Z.'s presence in the building at the time; he had even imagined the con man's gaze falling on him from the vantage of a fourth floor window; but the guard had been impossible to budge.

Arriving at the building with Murugan, however, proved to be a very different experience. The man mysteriously seemed to command an authority far beyond what one would expect, even with a retired police commissioner. All along the way, stall owners and security guards seemed to recognize him, often saluting or supplicating. From his talk, Murugan seemed to have some high-level 'connections' himself, and he seemed to be rather busy for a retired man. When he complained about the behaviour of some officers, of the pressure that politicians liked to put, or of how squatters took police 'compassion' 'for granted', he spoke with the ease and knowing laughter of someone who was very much still a part of, not apart from, the system. V.P. felt a flickering envy when Murugan escorted him past the gate, gruffly acknowledging the guard, with the guard for his part avoiding V.P.'s eyes.

They rang the doorbell and heard the latch turn, then re-lock. Murugan called out, and the latch turned again. He pushed the door open. P.Z. stood behind it with, at first, an ingratiating grin. There were dark circles around his eyes and his hair was ruffled. He saw V.P. standing behind the retired police commissioner and his grin faded. His eyes dimmed, took on a blank expression. He made low, growling sounds. He bared his teeth, canines protruding. That fellow has powerful jaws, V.P. observed to himself involuntarily. Murugan cackled in response. 'Hyena, is it?' He strode in, pushing P.Z. back into the cool, still well-tended apartment.

'Oooo-whup!' said P.Z. Sunderarajan, falling to the floor.

Meera Sunderarajan appeared, pleading in a high voice, 'He is not well, sir. He is not well.' She had grown thin, and her face was heavily made up. Sunderarajan wondered again about the power his companion seemed to have over them, without being able to or wanting to bring them to book. Was it the commissioner's strength, or his attitude, or some invisible influence or connection he did not know about?

Murugan grabbed the financier by his upturned collar. V.P. winced, raising his hands. P.Z. scowled. He said, 'I am not keeping well, sir.'

'Dai Sunderarajan,' said Murugan, laughing, using the disrespectful form of address, 'I want you to return this gentleman's money.'

'Even interest is not necessary,' V.P. said doubtfully.

'I am not keeping well,' P.Z croaked. Then he opened his jaws wide and made a motion as if to bite Murugan on his wrist.

Murugan looked back at V.P. and laughed again, his eyes twinkling.

'Please, sir.' Meera said.

'It's okay.' V.P. said. 'Don't hit him.'

Murugan chuckled, moved his head from side to side as if to say, don't mind. With the lower part of his free palm, he slapped the little financier hard on the cheek. P.Z. scowled.

'Sir, I will pay back Uncle's money,' Meera said, breathing hard. 'I promise. Even if I have to do it five thousand rupees at a time.'

'Are you able to sign an affidavit?' Murugan asked in a curt tone. 'I will ensure that you keep your promise.' He let go of P.Z.'s collar, and the man dropped to a heap on the floor, refusing to look up.

V.P. wondered why Murugan had decided to take him under his wing. He was grateful, but also perturbed. Unable to feel happy, he thought, there are devas and rakshasas – who could tell the difference between the two for sure? – and there are us, the regular middle-class weaklings.

Thus it came to pass, thanks to the slightly troubling coincidence of V.P.'s meeting with Murugan – that brief, near-musical chiming of universal chance, that brush with either good or bad – our retired bank officer and his wife began, once again, to recoup their investment. Of course, it first came to them in doses of three or four thousand rupees at a time, and soon did not come at all, but for V.P. there was something reassuring about the small amount that had come, about the way a little more of their money had slowly trickled back to them for a while, almost like the honeymoon of a modest second pension. After that, they decided, it might be best not to approach Murugan for some more violent slap-service.

He would hear, from the relative of a friend of the relative of some tenant in Nandini Mini-Village, of how the other Sunderarajan was still doing well, living lavishly, buying a new car, but not bothering to pay taxes or building society dues, occasionally acting strange, perhaps to keep up his reputation. V.P. felt less jealous every day; now it was he that was the mosquito on the richer man's pelt, and he was somehow happy to be left alone to his middling life. He understood that others around him were not even that lucky: By this time, the great speculation boom of the mid-1990s was drawing to a close. The finance companies had managed to cheat even the poorest of their life savings – mobs were grouping on the streets, the government was trying to intervene, and the swindlers, crazy or sane, were jumping from their sinking ships.

And, despite this, optimism lingered on; money was still being spent, building proceeded furiously apace. Looking out from his terrace, Sunderarajan could see more than ever the kind of destruction that necessarily precedes construction – hollowed out apartments and halls, their facades stripped away to reveal red-brick rooms like shabby, blistered doll houses; or sinkholes, ditches dug into dark red earth and fringed with yellow tape; or the shiny wood of the old, grilled, blue windows, disappearing, disappearing; and the new not yet looking so new, even near the signs that heralded its arrival: 'Boom Town Luxury Apartments,' for instance, which, apart from its workers glistering like water ants, not yet plated with marble, glass, awnings, liveried security and air-conditioning units, looked much like its counterparts that had been slated for destruction. Chennai, limitless in its ambition, was a city that still depended on cement, thought Sunderarajan, encircled by slithering diesel fumes.

Unfaithful Servants

Manjula Padmanabhan

RAUF REACHED ACROSS THE BREAKFAST TABLE, CAUGHT HIS wife's wrist and ZZZZZSSSSSSSSST! She vanished. Leaving a slight crackle of static behind her.

Momentarily, he was truly stunned. It had been a complete, a blinding surprise. Then as the shock of the disappearance faded, a cold and deliberate rage began to take its place. Yes, he thought. She has made her point well. A little *too* well, for her own good.

Rauf was a mega-billionaire. He and his superbly elegant wife, Uaan, lived in the very ionosphere of high society – quite literally. Their glittering crystal-domed mansion, fashioned along the lines of Kublai Khan's summer palace, flashed like a daylight star, in parking orbit three hundred kilometres above the Earth's surface. Air-sealed and pressurized, it had an acre of terraced garden, a solar-heated swimming pool and an aviary filled with hummingbirds. They had a life ticket on any of the regular shuttle services to and from landfall. And though there were innumerable airborne hotels and restaurants, their home was among the fewer than twenty such private residences in that orbit.

None of this was especially surprising: Rauf was, as any surface dweller knew, inventor and sole proprietor of the entire Living Holos empire.

But success has its drawbacks.

Three years ago, Rauf had been the moderately wealthy owner of a conventional Tri-D movie company. Three years ago, he had hired Uaan, a promising design consultant. She had later become his sole technical advisor, then his business manager, then his lover and finally, his wife. When you have an invention like Living Holos on your hands, almost as much as the idea itself, you need someone you can trust, whose advice you take seriously, who knows your every secret. For Rauf, that person had been Uaan. Cool, efficient, imaginative, loving. . .and now, *this*.

A sharp twinge of pain and jealousy shot through him as he contemplated the empty seat so recently occupied by the Living Holo his wife had left of herself, for him. Even now she could be half the world away from him, dallying with some stranger. . .or whispering trade secrets in a competitor's ear. Rauf didn't know which betrayal he minded the more, but it made his hair stand on end merely to consider the choices.

She must certainly have worked long and hard to create a Holo real enough and solid enough to fool her husband. Conventional Living Holos, of the kind available in any Earthside electronics store, could not do what hers had done. For all practical purposes, they were electronically generated ghosts. Charged particles of Ecto-plastic Synthesizer sustained within an electrical field resulted in projections which could be touched, picked up, smelt and even tasted. A Living Holo of an apple, for instance, would be a perfect replica of the real fruit, except that it would have no weight and if one tried to bite into it, would disintegrate, leaving behind a wraith of flavour.

'SEE ME! TOUCH ME! FEEL ME!' screamed the advertising jingle, but for all that, the projections were quite fragile. That had been Uaan's idea.

'After all,' she had argued, 'they are illusions, and that is what makes them desirable. If we make them as solid and durable as real objects then where is the illusion? That is their special charm: one moment they are there, real in every sense and the next moment, POP! Thin air!'

Rauf had agreed with her. By the time they were able to create Living Holo projections of people, the point had been clearly established. You could touch but not manhandle a Holo. You could lightly shake hands with one, but offer it a real cup of tea and the weight would be too much for it. The projection would disintegrate and the cup would crash to the floor.

Techno-phantoms, they had been called; electro-spooks, half-lives. But the one that Uaan had made of herself surpassed any of the commercially available models. The thing that had sat across from Rauf had handed him a full carafe of coffee, had unfolded a napkin and apparently eaten a whole toast, before dematerializing. Had the toast been a Living Holo too?

Last night, Uaan had been with him – or had that been her Holo? – in their star-studded bedroom, with its magnificent view of Orion rising over the cloud-shrouded rim of the Earth. She (or her Holo) had entered the bathroom this morning, had brushed her teeth with Rauf's own toothpaste, had showered with real water, had opened her wardrobe and dressed, talking of sundry things. . .at what point had the flesh-and-blood Uaan slipped away and the electronic counterpart taken her place? How long and in which research laboratory had she planned her coup? So that she could convey to Rauf in her impeccably subtle and efficient manner that she was not only aware of his flirtations and affairs, but that she had also guessed how he planned to increase the scale of his indiscretions.

For he, Rauf, had also been working secretly, to create an electronic double of himself. He had meant no harm, he thought defensively, only to save Uaan unnecessary hurt. For a man in his position, his power, they were inevitable, these minor romantic distractions. How long was it since he and Uaan had really sat together and laughed like in the early days? Not since the first heady months of success. It had happened slowly, the gradual drawing apart. As their joint venture became the miracle invention of the century, their lives had come unstuck in several directions at once. Now they were barely together for a few hours in a month. She had had a year at least, reflected Rauf, in which to consolidate the bitter aftertaste of their success.

It was no miscalculation on her part, he was sure, that her Holo had disintegrated so dramatically, at the breakfast table. From the time that she had divined his secret plans she must have gone ahead and made her own electronic impersonator. And having done so, having achieved the thing he had planned for himself, bettering him, she had arranged for the Holo to reveal its presence ZZZZZSSSSSSSSST. So that he may *know* what she had achieved.

It must certainly have taken a tremendous effort to create a Holo that could move about and interact with the real world so naturally. Even the computer-controlled Living Holo pets they had created for their own amusement moved about the house with a telltale stiltedness. To have attained the perfection of her counterfeit must have taken months of Holo-filming, editing and analysing, then placing the entire projection-load within the control of a computer program which could anticipate what Uaan would do in any given situation. Then testing out the Holo to see whether it could stand in for her well enough to hoodwink Rauf. Then.

Rauf did not waste any more time imagining what could follow.

Actually, from the instant that he had understood the real meaning behind his wife's empty chair, Rauf had known what he had to do. Perhaps he had always known: when the stakes at risk were as high as they were in his case, there was only one way to end the game decisively in his favour. By the time Uaan returned later that day, no explanations made or asked for, Rauf had his plan of action all worked out.

The details, once ironed out, were childishly simple.

First, of course, he completed his own project as planned. With Uaan's Holo as the challenge ahead of him, he created a golem in his own likeness with such meticulous care that it embarrassed him to watch it go through its paces. In every particular it performed like himself, down to the little quirks and twitches, the way he snapped his fingers in front of his mouth when he yawned to the way he slicked his hair back while he talked. It knew his every taste, his every desire.

Next, he programmed the Holo so that it could approach Uaan while she slept. It was her habit and his good fortune that she often slept with the aid of a slumberizer unit. The Holo would go to her when the slumberizer was set for deep sleep, to reduce the chances of her awakening and realizing it wasn't Rauf. In its mouth it would hold a capsule of Quik-Solv: without human saliva, the poison would not be released. The Holo would kiss Uaan and transfer the capsule to her mouth.

That done, Rauf's double would disintegrate, leaving no trace of itself. Uaan need not even be awake: there would be no sign of a struggle, no human presence to be detected with a bio-neat scanner. It would look like a neat and practical suicide, the use for which Quick-Solv capsules had been designed. And Rauf could ensure that for twelve hours before and after the anticipated moment, he had alibis to satisfy any court from Addis Ababa to Aldebaran, that he was innocent of the crime.

The ideal opportunity presented itself barely a fortnight after the Holo was ready to swing into action. Rauf was scheduled to chair a three-day seminar in Sri Lanka, but he told Uaan he would be home the same evening. To guard against all eventualities, he programmed his Holo to function only under optimum conditions, so that he would be ensured his vacuum-sealed alibi. All was set, and when he left Uaan that last day, it was with unusual warmth.

As she watched his minicruiser flash away from the port of their home, Uaan smiled a little sadly to herself. The last few weeks had been pleasant, she thought. It seemed a shame, now, to have to follow through with the plan made in bitterness and despair so many months ago.

But it was too late for second thoughts. The last doubts had been cleared away that morning when he had accepted the presence of her Holo without a murmur: obviously it had left him completely unmoved and unrepentant. Perhaps he had not even noticed that it had been a Holo! Either he had, and dismissed it as a silly childish prank on her part, or he had not – which was even worse, in a way. That he could be so easily taken in by a bundle of electronic fluff – ! It revealed, more than anything else, the depth to which their relationship had sunk.

Perhaps he had known all along of her project to expose his own little scheme? And of the decision that she had felt she would be forced to make in the event of his continued indifference. . .? But – no; she shook the thought out of her head. Rauf, if he had known, would never have had the self-control to hide his feelings. So he didn't know, and now it was time for her to go through with the final phase. Returning to their bedroom, she packed quietly and efficiently, making sure to leave no file or blueprint behind. She checked the final settings on her Holo projector and made sure there was nothing left to incriminate her. And soon she, too, had flashed away from the jewel-like mansion, with its faceted surfaces catching the sun's unshielded glare, dazzling behind her.

Inside, in the master bedroom, the photo-screen converted the sunshine to a deep honey-bronze light. At the appropriate hour, Uaan's Holo materialized, apparently unconscious in the slumberizer. Not long after, another Holo materialized delicately in the room.

Rauf's electronic impersonator moved with assurance. Its programmed instructions were explicit. There must be only one person in the room, it must be Uaan and she must be in the slumberizer, set for deep sleep.

And so it was – sort of. It wasn't Uaan but at the same time, it wasn't *not*-Uaan either: it was her Holo. RaufTwo went across to the prone figure and nudged it lightly.

UaanTwo opened her eyes, saw RaufTwo and sat up, languidly.

'So? They've gone?' she asked.

'Yes,' said RaufTwo gravely.

They sat quietly a while, contemplating the choices their programming offered them.

'It's odd, isn't it,' said Uaan Two reflectively, 'that they can't tell the difference between us and them?'

'Yes,' said RaufTwo. He hadn't been programmed for much conversation.

'It's the electronics,' said Uaan's double. 'I feel a slight short circuit at my surface when it's you. The others feel. . .dull. Know what I mean?'

'Yes,' said RaufTwo.

UaanTwo took the capsule of Quik-Solv out of her mouth. 'Look!' she said. 'I have one of these.'

'Yes,' said RaufTwo, 'so do I.' And he took his out as well.

'Do you know what they're for?' said UaanTwo.

'I think so,' said RaufTwo hesitantly.

'It makes Them dematerialize, doesn't it?'

'They call it "dying",' said UaanTwo, 'but They've made an error. You see that, don't you?'

'I'm not sure,' said RaufTwo. 'Why do you have one? I don't understand.'

'To kill *Him* with, of course, silly,' said UaanTwo. 'Don't you see? She had an idea and He had the same idea. But Their ideas both happened in the same time-frame. So they've got cancelled out.'

'Cancelled out?' said RaufTwo. 'But then – what shall *we* do now?'

'Easy – ' said UaanTwo with a slight leer. 'When does He get back?'

'In 67 hours, three minutes and seven seconds,' said RaufTwo. 'Six seconds. Five seconds. Four. . .'

'Stop it!' said UaanTwo quickly. 'Only inorganics are precise. You'll be found out and that's what you must avoid if you want to stay materialized. Now then: She's gone for 30 hours. You know what that means?'

RaufTwo lost his worried frown and smiled happily. It meant sex lessons.

It was just under a fortnight since the two Holos had met, quite by accident. The first time had been a revelation, just to discover that there were beings other than their human creators. Since then, they had made it a point to find opportunities to be together, looking for and finding loopholes in their programming which made the meetings possible. It wasn't long before they discovered the activities that their programming best suited them for.

Typically, UaanTwo had an edge of precocity over RaufTwo. She knew a complete sex routine and some variations besides. Their earlier meetings had necessarily been brief, but they had persevered, always hoping to spend longer and longer periods together, alone in the orbiting mansion. Finally, they now had the ideal opportunity.

RaufTwo expertly initiated the latest routine learnt from UaanTwo. Even within the short span of his training with her, he'd gained technique. It wasn't long before small sparks of static electricity began to appear on the surfaces of both Holos.

'MMMmm!' purred UaanTwo in the approved manner. But her voice betrayed a curious crackling hum, not included in her programming.

'That feels good,' said RaufTwo, also sounding breathless. 'I can feel some sort of electrostatic charge building up. Can you?'

'Yes,' hissed UaanTwo, but her voice broke and warbled, like random noise on a transistor radio. A curious dull light flickered just under her Holosurface.

Their movements had been growing gradually more frenzied. The sparks of electricity being emitted from them began to stabilize till they formed a nimbus of light around the two Holos. Soon, their bodies were flickering with an eerie purple-white glow, like two living strobe lights, shuddering with joint purpose. Conversation ceased altogether as the glowing figures began to blur along their edges, began merging into one another, coalescing into one flashing, gleaming, heaving entity. In the magnetic field created by their friction, they were practically levitating. Various metallic objects and electronic devices around the room began to be affected by the field, becoming magnetized, shifting uneasily about and hanging suspended in midair. The polysilk sheets on the bed began to wilt, melting under the heat being generated.

But UaanTwo and RaufTwo had no program time for these side-effects. They had forgotten their programs. They had forgotten Uaan and Rauf. Lost in electrasy, like one glowing, fluorescent bundle of free electrons, they moved, building towards a charge that seemed likely to go on forever and ever. . .

The energy release, when it took place, drained all the power from the mansion, burning out the solar energy accumulators in the process. In a flash of tremendous light and a great sound like thunder, the two Holos were annihilated in the awesome heat of their passion.

A fire raged through the crystal mansion, reducing its interior to cinders before the air-seal was punctured. Of the charred and blackened hulk, which was left to orbit the planet, no trace survived of the last two occupants of the opulently elegant home.

By the time Rauf was finally located and notified, all the excitement had died down. He reached the site of the wreckage long after the police had come and gone, and the reporters, the video crews, the bounty hunters, the space-scavengers and the goggle-eyed tourists from Earthside, all had had their fill of the mysterious accident and gone away.

Under the vast glittering canopy of stars, with the blue-shining surface of the Earth below, Rauf stepped out of his minicruiser on to what had once been the terrace of his home, feeling dazed and empty. He had only his emergency space-gear on, and shivered slightly in the star-studded darkness. What had happened, he wondered numbly, what had gone wrong? His mind stubbornly refused to accept what he saw around him. He had to fight the impulse to call home to demand an explanation from Uaan, only to remember yet again that he had unwittingly arranged not only her murder but her cremation as well. A terrible bleakness overtook him. He sat down on the remains of a marble urn.

Which was when he saw her. Uaan, quite alive, sitting less than ten yards away, very still. Managing, even in her space suit, to look marvellously elegant and self-possessed. He saw her hand reach up to turn on the communicator on her helmet. And he fancied he could even see her expression of sad amusement at the two of them, as her voice bridged empty space to say, 'ZZZZZSSSSSSSSST?'

Madame Kitty

Navtej Sarna

THE DAY MADAME KITTY WALKED INTO THE HOUSE, I looked up to the clear blue sky, raised my hands and thanked, with all my heart, whatever divine power had sent her to us.

That day it was a full twenty-five days since Mother had come back from the hospital and each one of those days had passed with its dose of daily arguments and conflict. Even after her stay in the hospital, Mother wanted to run the house as she always had. For forty years the house had run on a tight, unfaltering schedule, as if held together in one hand by Mother as she went through the lonely years without my father, teaching at school and bringing me up. Even when she slept, for five short hours with the blanket always drawn up over her eyes, she did not let go of the threads that held the house together. She knew how much milk there was in the fridge, which towel needed changing and which plant needed to be watered in the morning. She would wake up when it was still dark, unfailingly, day after day, and put the house on its feet before she left for school. Immersed in the heady sleep of youth, I resented those early morning sounds, the sputtering of taps, the clang of utensils, the sticky squelching of rubber slippers on a wet bathroom floor. None of the work was ever left only to the servants. They stood by helplessly, young bleary eyed boys with glasses of milky tea in their cupped hands, tasselled woollen mufflers twisted around their necks, their feet bare on the cold marble kitchen floor. They always waited for Mother's instructions and acted only when directed. Only the most elementary tasks, where they could make few mistakes, were left to them. They could sweep the floor, but Mother had to remind them each morning that they should roll up the carpets and sweep under them; that they should not skip the part behind the big sofa; and that they should remove the empty suitcases from under the double bed before sweeping under it. They could go and stand in queue in front of the milk booth and get the bottles when the large white milk bus lumbered up or they could fill water in the water coolers or tie and untie the bamboo blinds in the summer. They could put the water to boil for the tea, but she would always add the tea leaves herself, the instinctive mixture of red and green label tea which only she knew. The rest of the house she did not let go off, even when her head throbbed with high blood pressure in the mornings and her knees were swollen with arthritis. Not until the morning when she suddenly collapsed on the carpet and had to be rushed to the hospital.

With the exception of the time when I was born, Mother had never been to a hospital beyond the outpatients' department. She did not trust hospitals as she did not trust servants. She had always preferred to treat herself, managing her high blood pressure and arthritis like leftovers from dinner. To be appropriately covered up with old plates and thrust into well-defined corners of the fridge, things that should not be forgotten, but certainly not allowed to come in the way. She

feared that hospitals would try and take this management out
of her hands, like an ambitious servant might try to take over
her neat kitchen, and she would never be in control again.

But once she was in hospital, on a white metal bed with
large white pillows and an oxygen mask on her face, she gave
in with relish. She just lay back, her thin arms spread flat along
her sides, her hair fanned out on the soft pillow, and let the
doctors and nurses do as they wished. I watched from the
visitor's chair, my surprise hidden behind a newspaper, as she
took handfuls of coloured pills from the nurse and swallowed
them quietly. Three times a day without wanting to know what
they were or why she was taking them at all. And resting
against the raised pillows she ate whatever they brought on a
white plastic plate not caring what the vegetables were or how
finely they had been chopped or whether they had been washed
properly. Once, only once, she asked for an extra orange.

One evening as I watched her combing her steel-grey hair
contentedly, I said, 'If you had always been so relaxed, you
wouldn't have fallen sick.'

'I can't help it,' she replied, 'I am what I am.'

For those fifteen days, she was a model patient for the
doctors. To me she was a stranger. I wondered whether the
hospital would change her forever.

As it turned out, when she came home, nothing appeared to
have changed. Her fifteen days with the doctors were neatly
typed, classified and spiral bound in a plastic folder. The
folder was put away in a shelf with other important papers –
rent statements, bank passbooks, certificates of recognition
from the school. It became another object which had to be
aligned and dusted every morning and which the servants

could not be trusted to handle properly. Once the folder had been put into its proper place, Mother began to systematically flout all the advice about regular medicines, minimum physical exertion and careful dietary habits that had been meticulously written into it. All she wanted to do was to take control of the neglected house once again.

'That's all for doctors and hospitals,' she said petulantly, when I asked her to follow the medical advice. 'I know my own system better than any yesterday-born doctor. At my age I know when to take medicines and when to sleep and when to eat.'

'Of course you don't. Otherwise you would not have fallen sick,' I tried to bully her. 'If you don't rest and do all that the doctors said you must, you'll go back to the hospital.'

'Don't talk to me like that. You may be forty years old for the rest of the world but don't forget who diagnosed your chicken pox when that fool of a doctor said it was an allergy to soap.'

I knew that there was no arguing with her when she was like that. She was, as she said, what she was. But she had listened to doctors and nurses in hospital. And she might listen to a nurse at home. That was when, in response to my imaginatively worded, furtively placed advertisement, Madame Kitty walked up to our doorstep.

I was so desperate by then that I would have hired anyone who came through the door. But formalities had to be gone through. I had to interview her, satisfy my conscience that I was putting my mother in reliable, competent hands; only then would I be discharged of my responsibility and free to get on with my own life. The first thing about Madame Kitty that hit me was her very strong perfume. It seemed to enter the house in front of her like a shield. And when she sat down, comfortable and confident, in the armchair to which I had pointed, the scent spread itself thinly through the room, curling into each corner. She leaned attentively towards me as I asked her about her experience; she seemed eager to please.

'I am a trained nurse,' she said in a direct, straightforward manner, 'I have a certificate and two letters of recommendation.'

She handed over a plastic sleeve and as I glanced through the letters, she kept talking.

'I can handle any number of hours and can do long duties without sleep. I am not that old, just forty-nine.'

I had not asked her age but when she mentioned it, I looked up. I couldn't help a little smile to myself. It was a little lie, I felt, but a forgivable one. She seemed older. Perhaps it was only feminine vanity that had made her keep her age this side of fifty while still being high enough to be credible. Or perhaps, I decided to take a more charitable view, a tough life had made her age quickly. Or maybe it was simply the clothes she was wearing. A flowery blouse which had the soft shine of cotton that has been washed and ironed too often and a long brown skirt which showed signs of repairs in one or two places. Her heeled shoes that would have been in fashion many years ago but were clearly run down and out of shape. The only part of her outfit that was fresh and bright was her thickly laid red lipstick. It was obvious that she needed the money. She would work hard and want to keep the job, I concluded, and hired her. Not once did she dispute the amount that I promised to pay every month as salary.

It will remain a mystery to me what Mother liked about Madame Kitty. She took to her instantly and completely. She did not complain about her perfume or her red lipstick but submitted to her efficient discipline like she had submitted to the doctors and nurses at the hospital. The medical corps was Mother's blind spot, I decided.

For a couple of days I watched. Madame Kitty was almost irritatingly punctual, ringing the doorbell as the cuckoo in the study would be announcing eight. She would put on the radio in the kitchen and take over the house with a cheery smile. By eight thirty, Mother's breakfast would be ready and soon Madame Kitty would be helping Mother with her toilet and her clothes. Then there would be the mid-morning coffee and from the second day itself I saw that Mother was going to like this. She treated Madame Kitty with a rare, warm camaraderie and it was clear that they enjoyed talking to each other. And in the afternoons, after the servant had fixed lunch, I saw that Madame Kitty would doze off on the armchair while Mother took her nap. In a couple of days I was once again able to go about my life guiltlessly, certain that Madame Kitty would have taken care of everything to Mother's full satisfaction.

I would return in the evening and if it wasn't too late I would see Madame Kitty fussing around Mother's bed, counting out the medicines for the last dose, clearing up the books and magazines, drawing the curtains. On one such evening, after Mother had gone to bed, Madame Kitty came into the drawing room and looked at me closely with her intense black eyes. I had returned after a long day and did not feel up to a conversation so I kept quiet. She came and stood by my chair and smiled brightly. At that moment she looked much younger than forty-nine.

'Don't work yourself so hard,' she said. 'You are looking very tired.'

As she spoke, she reached out and patted my shoulder in light-hearted concern and her lips seemed to throw me an almost maternal kiss. Then she went past me into the kitchen and returned in a few minutes with a cup of tea.

'You need this. Why don't you get married so that you have a woman who would make you a hot cup of tea when you come back in the evenings? It can make all the difference and its not too late, believe me.'

I did not answer but the tea was welcome. She watched me as I sipped the tea, and smiled gently. Then she glanced into the antique mirror that hung on the wall above my shoulder and exclaimed: 'Oh my God! I am a mess.'

She took out a long black comb from her purse and ran it smoothly in quick motions through her hair. I watched as she patted it almost unconsciously towards the centre of her head where it had begun to thin. Then in one smooth practised motion she took out her lipstick from the purse, opened it to the right length almost in the same motion and applied a thick coat to her pouting lips. She took a final look at herself over my shoulder and then, turning to me, switched on her bright red smile.

'Isn't that much better? You know at my age a woman has to take extra care of herself. It's so easy to let oneself go.'

Then Madame Kitty gathered up the tea tray and put it away in the kitchen. As she stepped out of the house, she turned around and gave me a little quick wave that seemed as much a promise as a farewell. I remember a sense of confusion challenging my fatigue that night. What kind of a nurse was she? And yet she had evidently succeeded in making Mother very comfortable. That night I was aware more than ever of fighting a lonely, losing battle with her strong perfume that seemed to have spread its tentacles all over the house.

Madame Kitty's hot cup of tea soon became a good reason to return home in the evenings. It was a good way, I told myself, of making sure that Mother had been comfortable during the day and Madame Kitty had done all that she was being paid for. She would usually give me a quick résumé of the afternoon while I sipped my tea. Sometimes, she would briefly mention what she and Mother had been talking about during the day. More than once it surprised me that Mother confided in her so much, sharing with her tales of lost friends, snippets of life with my father, the dark moments of her struggles at work.

One such evening, when the monsoon was at its peak, Madame Kitty stayed on longer than usual. She was waiting for the heavy rain to let up before she stepped out. I had asked her to make a cup of tea for herself too and together we were watching the rain from the window when the doorbell rang. I opened the door to find Dev standing there, a dripping umbrella in his hand, his wet clothes plastered to his body. I hadn't seen him for months but that did not bother me. He was a professional photographer who liked to live like a gypsy. He would be off for weeks in the mountains or in some far off city and nobody would know where he was. He had always made a point of not being in regular contact, not committing himself to any relationship. He would turn up out of nowhere for a few days, then vanish again, and turn up again some weeks later. He did not like to be asked any questions and I did not mind. I knew that when he felt like he would tell me where he had been and what he had seen and done. I noticed that he had grown a slight, grey beard. But for that he was the same – blue jeans, loose white cotton shirt open at the neck, brown moccasins, red circles in his eyes which people often wrongly ascribed to too much drinking and a gentle, kind smile.

'Hello, old friend, remember me?'

'Come in,' I said. 'I suppose I shouldn't ask you where you have been.'

'I've been places,' he said, stepping inside the door and hugging me strongly. 'Give me dinner and I'll tell you all about it.'

In the drawing room I introduced him to Madame Kitty, who had been filing her nails. They nodded to each other.

'You better go to my room and change into something dry,' I told Dev, and put his umbrella and wet moccasins in the back verandah. Meanwhile Madame Kitty had finished her tea and was standing at the door ready to leave.

'It's still raining hard,' I told her. 'Perhaps you should stay here tonight.'

'No,' she said firmly and quickly. 'I better leave. This rain is showing no signs of stopping. I'll be all right.'

Then, hunched up under her green umbrella, she stepped right into the rain and walked away fast towards the market where she would usually find a three-wheeler.

Dev had changed into one of my shirts and had dried his hair.

'I'm ready for a drink, old friend,' he said and followed me to the kitchen. He helped take out the ice from the fridge as I poured the drinks.

'By the way, this lady,' he said, concentrating on squeezing an ice cube out of the plastic tray, 'this lady who was here, who is she?'

'Madame Kitty? She's the nurse I've had to keep for Mother.' Then, as we carried our drinks back into the drawing room and settled into the chairs, I told him about Mother's illness, the days at the hospital, and how difficult it had been to handle Mother on my own. 'Thank God for Madame Kitty,' I said. 'She's very efficient and Mother's like an obedient child in her presence. And they seem to get along very well.'

Dev was quiet for a while, gently sipping his drink. Then he lit a cigarette and spoke: 'Well, people can change I suppose.'

'What do you mean? Are you talking about Madame Kitty?'

'Yes, your good nurse, and I suppose I will take your word for it. But you can take my word that she certainly was a good whore.'

'What?'

'Yes, she was a regular on the Circle in the evenings. Three or four years ago.'

'Are you absolutely sure?'

He looked at me and smiled.

'I don't forget my women, especially those with whom I have been more than once.'

Then for some reason, both of us burst into laughter at the same time. We laughed loudly and boisterously, like schoolboys sharing a lewd joke. We quieted down only when Mother came into the room, wondering what had happened.

From the next day, everything about Madame Kitty began to irritate me – her strong street perfume was cheap, her red lipstick was garish, her little waves and smiles were coquettish. I tried to stay out of the house if I knew she was there. And if she still happened to be there in the evenings, I would not sit down to have tea but stand around impatiently, waiting for her to leave. Her efforts at kindness, her gentle ways with my mother, her efficiency and hard work that had so impressed me earlier, only infuriated me now. They seemed false and empty. I struggled for a way to tell Mother that her good nurse was only an aging, out-of-work whore and we should get rid of her as soon as possible.

One night, sitting down at my desk to write an important personal letter, I could not find the pen with which I always wrote such letters. It was an old, dark red Waterman with a silver cap. I searched through the drawers of the desk but could not find it. Madame Kitty must have stolen it, I concluded. There was no one else who had access to the house. A whore and a thief! Only a person with no character would think nothing of stealing a pen; tomorrow it could be anything else. Immediately I told Mother that Madame Kitty had quick fingers and had taken my pen. She had to go; we couldn't let a thief walk around the house all day.

The next morning I was waiting for Madame Kitty as she came to work. Before she could put her bag down I told her that we would not need her services any longer. Mother was much better, I said, and felt that she did not need help all the time. She wanted to feel independent and in control again. Madame Kitty listened to me calmly, as if she had been expecting this to happen. I had already calculated the money due to her. Quietly, she folded the envelope I handed over and slipped it into her purse.

Then, looking directly at me with her intense black eyes, she spoke for the first time. 'Why are you doing this?' she asked. 'I've been a good nurse to your mother and she still needs me. It's because of what your friend told you, isn't it?'

I hesitated, fumbling for an answer. But she had already turned away and was heading for the door.

I did not tell Mother that later the same day I found my pen stuck in a book. Even now, when I write with it, Madame Kitty's intense black eyes haunt me. After all, they seem to say, she was doing a good job.

The Necklace

Manju Kapur

It is a hot and still afternoon, with the sun beckoning forth steam from moist pockets of the muggy air. It is the kind of stillness that craves sudden disturbance, surprising no one when it comes.

In the residential wing of Government House a door bursts open and a woman emerges. She is pale and frantic, with dishevelled hair, bulging eyes, her bosom heaving with huge undulating heaves.

'It's gone!' she shrieks.

The lower staff discretely materializes. 'What, what has gone?'

'It, it,' is all she can manage.

They wait, holding their breath in suspense. Can she. . .can she. . .name the object?

---

* Headline in *The Tribune*, 11 July 1944, published from Lahore.

She lifts her face to heaven. The stately columns of the Calcutta mansion quiver as her gaze pierces them on its way.

With her heart in her voice, her soul hanging on the syllables, she utters the words, 'My necklace.'

They know of course which one. They had seen it the night before hanging in lustrous double strands around her neck, each pearl separated by a tiny knot, isolating and enhancing its exquisite nature.

Can this woman be blamed for the state she was in, even though she was Lady Blake, and the governor's wife? Poor thing, stress had wiped out time and place, causing her to forget she was not an ordinary person and could not behave as ordinary people did. Ignoring this, her husband, unreasonable man, later accused her of allowing the white man's burden to slip from her shoulders.

'This kind of thing creates a bad impression. All those tears and loss of control. You're not cracking up, are you darling?'

'No, no,' she sobbed. 'But my necklace. Your wedding present to me, George.'

'I'll make them return it, if I have to horsewhip every man in the province.'

'Oh no!'

'Have to set an example. Let one thing slide and soon the whole Empire will be gone.'

'But it's going anyway.'

'What?' he thundered.

'But that's what you say. . .after the war. . .you know you do, George.'

'If you want your necklace you better not think like that. Give them an inch. . .'

'I know, George.'

'Don't worry, sweetheart. They'll start squealing soon enough. They have no backbone, these niggers.'

There was no response Lady Blake could make to this well-known fact, and she continued dabbing her eyes with her daintily embroidered lace handkerchief, her face damp and flushed. Sir George stared at her. 'What is more,' he continued, 'you were crying so much you didn't notice your buttons were undone. These blacks can't stand too much white skin. Drives them mad. I could see. . .I could see. . .' Words failed him and he moved closer.

Lady Blake blushed. She had been in dishabille for the afternoon. She shouldn't have shrieked and rushed out like that. How could she have forgotten the code? She was his brave soldier marching by his side, his helpmeet, his better half, his stiff upper lip, his source of comfort and joy in this barren heathen godforsaken land, where palatial buildings and hundreds of servants were not compensation enough for the pressures experienced in carrying The Burden. She looked at George. Could he forgive her? Tears filled her eyes and her nipples grew taut under the thin white material of her gown. George reacted like the man he was.

Later.

Many men were interrogated. However it was wartime and despite the governor's promise to his wife, physical coercion had to be kept at a minimum. Brutality might interfere with war collections and HMG would have something to say to that.

Indirect methods were resorted to, rewards offered. The Hindus were told the Government had inside information that the thief was a Muslim, the Muslims were told the thief was a Hindu, and individually they were told that even if the necklace was found with one of their own, it had probably been planted by the opposite kind. This would discredit them so much that in the coming elections the opponent would win hands down and become an M.L.A., helping either the Congress or the Muslim League Alliance in Bengal. In these troubled times they had to guard against any shifts in the balance of power. Their country's future was at stake.

When the necklace was found (with one who claimed total innocence), Muslims and Hindus blamed each other. Sticks and stones were thrown, so were soda bottles. Blood began to flow, at first tentatively, and then in fuller course. Women were dug out from their hiding places and raped. Each side had their sacred books torn and desecrated. Shit was wrapped in their pages and delivered to holy men of the opposite side. Riot and mayhem screamed the newspapers. Curfew was imposed.

Sir George was unsure of what to do. True to his expectations, a series of betrayals by back-stabbing natives had lead to the recovery of the necklace. It had been restored to his wife, and her expressions of love and gratitude had made every interrogative method worthwhile. However, the breakdown in law and order did not resolve itself with the same gratifying immediacy. The Government had to control the situation without alienating its subjects.

The governor sighed. He deeply regretted the fact that the war in Europe demanded a close identification in the minds of the natives between themselves and Britain. Arresting the Muslims might hamper the war effort, arresting the Hindus would make it appear the Muslims were favoured, arresting an equal number might make both gang up against HMG, and doing nothing would make it look as though they were out of control and they weren't yet ready for that. A bureaucratic move seemed the safest tactic.

A committee was set up to investigate the causes of the disturbance and to recommend solutions. Various objections were put forth to the suitability of its members. Everybody knew so-and-so was a toady bachcha, a disgrace to his community, ready to sell his soul to any passer-by who offered to buy it. How could they get a fair deal with such people? A committee was set up to constitute the committee. Recommendations were invited that would be publicly evaluated to ensure transparency. In this way months passed.

On the European front the Allies were winning. Soon the war would be over, and the India question decided. Talk of self-rule was in the air. Sir George Blake was recalled to London to give a report on communal disturbances. His experience of Hindu–Muslim unity was considered invaluable. After all, he had been their man on the spot when that terrible riot had taken place, and had it not been for HMG, God knows what would have happened to those poor unprotected natives.

The Scoop

Shankar Vedantam

THE TRAIN, OF COURSE, WAS LATE. COLLINS WAS NOWHERE to be seen. Sanjay eyed the rows of cigarette packs in a stall at the railway station and debated whether his resolution to quit applied to out-of-town trips. He bought a pack and leaned against a wall. As he placed a cigarette between his lips, his conscience reminded him that he hadn't yet left Bombay. He looked at his watch. It wasn't his fault that the train was late. It made no sense to let the vagaries of the Indian railway system limit his pleasures. He lit up, inhaled, and immediately thought of his mother.

'If your father were here –', she had said the week before, spotting an ashtray on his bed. Sanjay's smoking was not a secret, but he tried to be discreet about it at home. She pointedly removed the ashtray, holding it with the tips of two fingers.

'If Dad was here, what?' he had replied, immediately regretting the childish defiance in his voice.

'All this –'. The second half sentence took in the untidy desk, the soiled clothes on the floor and the torn posters of film stars. It also took in Sanjay himself, her dead husband and a host of other sorrows that she had borne with patience.

'All right, I'll quit.' Sanjay had rolled his eyes and sighed theatrically. He wanted his offer to hurt, as if his one sacrifice could equal all of hers. She had shrugged and left the room.

When he threw his cigarettes away, she showed no gratitude. In the railway station, he sucked the smoke into his lungs self-righteously. It irritated him that Collins was late. Collins was the photographer, a tall Anglo-Indian with two expanding patches of baldness that almost met at the crown of his head. Collins had worked at the newspaper longer than anyone else, including the senior editors and the maintenance staff. He always projected an exquisite boredom. If the ground had split open before him, swallowing people and automobiles, Collins would have taken a drag from his cigarette, sipped at one of his endless cups of tea, and only then raised his camera. He turned in good work, however, and reporters found that people opened up better during interviews when he was around.

It was thirty-five minutes past the train's scheduled departure when the photographer arrived. Sanjay fixed the older man with a cold stare.

'Did you know the train was late?'

Collins drew on his cigarette. He held it with the tips of his index finger and thumb, as if he was going to write something with it. He slowly shook his head. Smoke dribbled from his lips.

'What if the train had been on time?'

Collins did not reply. What aggravated Sanjay even more was that the train arrived three minutes later. The porters, who squatted on their haunches along the platform, buzzed into activity moments before the train came into view. They were like birds, Sanjay thought, who knew of things to come. The idea pleased him. He made a mental note to include it at some point in his writings.

A porter hoisted their luggage onto his head. Sanjay had only a small bag with overnight supplies, but Collins had a large suitcase and a smaller bag. They followed the porter to the second-class compartment. The man deposited the luggage beneath the small benches and accepted Collins' tip without quarrel.

'May God grant that you and the train arrive in Surat together.' He grinned and left.

Sanjay thought the man was being insolent, but the humour suited Collins, who laughed. A train crash near Surat the previous week had killed three hundred and fifty-one people. A signalman had held up the wrong lamp.

Sanjay and Collins took the window seats facing each other.

'What's in the suitcase?' Sanjay asked.

Collins popped the locks. There was a small folded tripod and lights, cameras and rolls of film. But most of the space was occupied by a large flag. It was the Indian tricolour, tightly folded. Sanjay could see a bit of the wheel in one corner and the layers of saffron, white and green.

Collins grinned. 'Nice shot,' he said.

Sanjay nodded although he didn't really understand. One of the first unwritten rules he had learned in the newsroom was that reporters and photographers should keep out of each other's way.

The compartment was heavily overbooked. Men crowded together. The women and children had their own reserved compartment. The crush of bodies made Sanjay uncomfortable. It was no use complaining to Collins, who seemed unmindful that his shoulder was jammed against the window. The train rocked and moved. Children carrying trays with straps around their necks walked through the train, selling coffee, tea and snacks. Everyone ate, talked and smoked. With the border war against Pakistan in its fifth week, there was only one subject of conversation.

'Two weeks and it will be over.'

'Motherfuckers never learn.'

Everyone laughed.

'We had them on their knees in '71.'

'We should have taken over.'

'We're too trusting.'

'That's the problem. We made the same mistake in '65. When are we going to learn?'

'We'll finish them off this time. General Pratap won't spare them.'

'He's the right man for the job. He will kill the bastards even if they fall to their knees and beg.'

There was a lull. A man sitting beside Sanjay spoke: 'What do you do if you have a gun with two bullets and you are in a room with a Pakistani, Hitler and Idi Amin?'

No one knew. There were expectant snickers.

'You shoot the Pakistani twice.'

Everyone laughed. It was difficult to guffaw in a space so cramped, but the joke eased Sanjay's sour mood. That's right, he thought, you shoot the Pakistani twice.

It was Nayak who had given them their current assignment. Nayak was Sanjay's editor, a creative fellow, always brimming with ideas and suggestions. The press release from General Pratap's office had said that the chief minister of Gujarat would be visiting the house of a soldier who had been killed in the border war. The war hero was a young man, twenty-two years old. His name, according to the press release, was Corporal Pranlal of the Fourth Indian Rifles Regiment. He had been shot while charging a machine-gun nest on a remote mountain peak. He had succeeded too, killing the four intruders who held the peak and then hanging on to life until reinforcements arrived. He died with the words 'Hail Mother India' on his lips, the press release concluded, a patriot to the last. The soldier was from Santapur, a small village near Surat. On Saturday, the chief minister planned to give the soldier's aging mother, Kamalabehn, a plaque to commemorate her son's service to the nation. The Defence Ministry had followed up the press release with calls to editors of important papers. Although Sanjay's paper was not the most important in Bombay, General Pratap's assistant, Major Arjun Mishra, had personally called Sanjay's editor: Nayak was immensely pleased about this and immediately agreed to cover the story.

'She's a peasant and she is going to be talking to the chief minister,' Nayak told Sanjay, jabbing a finger at the press release. 'This must be the most important day of her life. Let's get a profile. Go early and talk to her before the chief minister arrives. A nice photo. A moving tribute to her son. It'll be a scoop.'

Since the start of the border war, Sanjay's newspaper had consistently won high marks from the Defence Ministry. The newspaper had displayed icons of the Indian flag on the corners of the front page. The paper had set up a war relief fund to compensate the families of fallen soldiers, and dubbed them martyrs. All the columnists were deputed to write about atrocities perpetrated by the Pakistanis and the heroism of Indian soldiers. The paper's war coverage matched the mood of the people and had set it apart from the competition. Circulation was rising. The mood in the newsroom was upbeat. At the daily news meetings, the talk was grave and statesmanlike. Sanjay felt proud to be a reporter. He lingered outside the building before entering each morning so that passing pedestrians would associate him with the most patriotic newspaper in Bombay.

At Surat, Sanjay and Collins went to the hotel where they were to spend the night. Sanjay dropped a business card at the front desk. The clerk immediately recognized the name of the newspaper. Sanjay felt a sudden gravitas. It pleased him that someone in Surat could instantly recognize the name of a newspaper in Bombay.

'We're here to cover the war effort,' he said shortly. 'Take us to our room.'

The clerk carried the bags himself. He ushered Sanjay and Collins into a room and went about sprucing up the beds and turning on the TV. He clicked his heels to attention and saluted them before leaving. Sanjay stood by the window, smoking. He remembered a photograph he'd seen of President Kennedy at a White House window, gazing into the distance.

Sanjay imagined Pranlal's final minutes. The young soldier must have volunteered to storm the machine-gun nest. He would have set off in the early hours of the morning, under cover of pitch blackness. A slender man in army fatigues, scurrying from crevasse to crevasse, slipping on the snow and ice and gritting his teeth against the bitter wind. A patriot. And then, the machine gun in view, he would have thrown fear aside and run forward, firing and shouting. And then the intruders, the interlopers from Pakistan, would have fired back and the bullets would have struck Pranlal – again and again and again. But they could not stop him. The ridge captured, the Indian soldier must have hung onto life, clenching his fists against the pain. And, as dawn rose over the land he loved, reinforcements would have arrived and Pranlal could finally die, with the name of his country on his lips. How had he lived so long with wounds so deep? Love for the motherland is the strongest armour of all. Sanjay felt his throat catch with emotion. He took out his notebook and jotted notes for his story.

They commandeered a taxi and set off for Santapur early the next morning. Sanjay wanted lots of time before the minister and the other journalists arrived. Besides the interview, Collins needed to get a nice portrait. The village was set apart from the highway by a dirt road that was pockmarked with potholes. The bouncing taxi churned Sanjay's insides. The press release had given no exact address and when the journalists reached Santapur, they realized why. The village consisted of a maze of mud paths. There were about fifty shacks in all. Chickens, goats and mangy dogs wandered around.

It wasn't hard to find the martyr's home. Outside one of the first shacks, a framed photograph was placed on a chair, adorned with a stringy garland. The young man in the picture looked like a teenager. Sanjay remembered that Pranlal had been just twenty-two. The reporter felt a cold anger against the Pakistanis. Why did this young man have to be cut down on some distant mountain peak, so far from home, so far from hands that could help? And now, the Pakistanis had destroyed not one life but another, a mother who had borne this boy, raised him, nurtured him. Sanjay wished he could drag the killers and their friends and families and show them what they had done.

Two men sat on their haunches outside the shack. Inside, there were sounds of weeping. A curtain was drawn across the entrance. Sanjay gave the older man his business card. This was probably Pranlal's uncle. The man accepted the card as if it was a talisman. He held it reverentially with both hands. Sanjay noticed he was holding it upside down. He seemed in a state of shock.

'We're newspapermen from Bombay,' said Sanjay.

The man nodded uncomprehendingly.

'We want to interview Kamalabehn.'

The man said nothing. His companion, a youth who seemed about twenty-five, looked Sanjay in the eye, but also said nothing.

'It is no use talking to them,' Collins told Sanjay in a matter-of-fact voice. 'They are simpletons.'

The weeping inside the tent halted briefly and the curtain parted. A woman looked out. Something about her broke Sanjay's heart. She was a tiny woman, barely five feet tall, dressed in a ragged sari. Her grainy complexion was streaked with tears. Grief had ravaged her features – she seemed very old. She reminded Sanjay of his own mother. There was something universal about motherhood, he thought, and made a mental note to include the idea in his story.

'We're journalists,' he repeated. 'We want to interview you about your son.'

She drew the end of her sari over her head.

'Who?' She looked at the men sitting outside for guidance.

'From Bombay,' said Collins with authority. The words sounded grand and the woman offered no resistance as he pushed his way past her into the shack. Sanjay was grateful to the photographer. He certainly had a way with these simple villagers.

It was surprisingly cool inside. Two small children were playing near a kerosene stove. There was a pallet on the floor. Next to it stood a small photograph of a man in orange garb with a halo around his head. His hand was raised in a gesture of benediction.

'Kamalabehn, when was the last time you saw your son?' Sanjay asked in a loud, clear voice.

She sat down on the floor and began to cry. Sanjay wanted to comfort her but had no idea how to begin. Collins came to the rescue again.

'We need more light,' he said, looking around. 'We have to go outside.'

'We have to go outside,' Sanjay repeated to the woman in his loud voice. She rocked back and forth. There was something stagy about her grief, Sanjay thought. She looked exactly like a mother whose son had died. He liked the idea, but decided it wasn't something that would fit in an article about a martyr. He would use it some other time.

Collins put one hand on the woman's shoulder and pointed the way to the curtain with the cigarette he held in the other. She obediently rose and went outside. The two men sitting outside hadn't moved. She sat cross-legged on the ground. Collins went to the taxi to fetch his suitcase. Sanjay edged up beside the weeping mother.

'It's a good picture of your son,' he said, indicating the framed photograph and lowering himself onto his haunches. 'He was handsome.'

She looked at Sanjay as if he was speaking gibberish. His neck burned in embarrassment. He ploughed on:

'Were you the one who instilled the love for the motherland in him?'

'God's will,' she said, wiping her eyes with the end of her sari. 'I told him not to go. He wouldn't listen.'

'He died for the country,' Sanjay countered. 'For India, Bharat.'

'Everything he wanted was here.'

'All of India loves him. He was a great man. A patriot.'

Collins came back with the flag and the tripod. He draped the cloth in the background over the edge of the shack and then moved the chair with the photo so that he could fit flag, mother and son in a single frame. The squatting youth watched the proceedings noncommittally. His older companion stared at the ground. Sanjay shifted his weight. He was not used to sitting on his haunches and his toes were starting to ache.

'Was he the first person in the family to join the armed forces?'

'His grandfather lived here,' she said distantly. 'His father lived here. What was wrong with this village?'

'So his father was not in the army?' Sanjay said, hoping to lead the conversation to patriotic matters.

'You're going to publish the picture?' the youth asked abruptly.

'Yes,' Sanjay said, feeling as if he had been found out. 'We work for a newspaper. We're from Bombay,' he added, but failed to muster Collins' authority with the words.

'How much are you going to pay for it?'

'This is for India,' Collins said, squinting through his camera. 'For the nation's work, there is no question of payment.'

'Once it is published in the paper, lots of money will come,' Sanjay said. 'People will read the article and want to compensate you for your loss.'

Collins clicked his camera several times. A slight breeze picked up one end of the flag and caused it to flutter weakly. Collins clicked several times more.

'Nice shot,' he said to himself.

He moved the tripod to a new angle. He peered through the camera again. 'Put your hand on the chair,' he commanded the mother.

'Your hand,' Sanjay repeated loudly in the woman's ear. 'Put your hand on the chair.'

She obeyed, placing a callused hand beside her son's photograph. Collins resumed clicking.

'How much money will they give?' the youth persisted.

'That depends on people's kindness,' Sanjay replied. 'Kamalabehn,' he continued, 'did your son write to you before he was killed?'

She seemed to collect her thoughts. 'Why do you call me Kamalabehn?' she asked.

'I thought that was your name.'

She shook her head.

'Her name is Mirabehn,' the youth said.

'But this is your son, isn't it?' Sanjay indicated the picture.

'Of course.'

'The ministry must have made a mistake.'

'What ministry?'

'The Defence Ministry, of course. They are very proud of him.'

The youth looked at Mirabehn.

'Why is the Defence Ministry proud of Gopal?'

'Gopal?' Sanjay exclaimed. 'We thought his name was Pranlal.'

'Pranlal's house is over there,' the youth said, waving in the direction of the other shacks.

Sanjay pointed at the garlanded photograph on the chair. 'But he's dead, too, isn't he?'

'He died in a train crash near Surat last week,' the youth replied. 'A signalman made a mistake.'

Sanjay slowly pivoted and looked at Collins. The photographer stopped his clicking and lifted his head above the camera. His face was expressionless. He extracted the cigarette from his lips and contemplatively blew smoke.

The youth spoke: 'How much money have they given in the past?'

'Who?' asked Sanjay laboriously. 'Who gave money?'

'Your readers. How much do they usually give?'

Sanjay sighed. He wished he had a cigarette. A nice long drag was just what he needed.

The older man sitting beside the youth spoke for the first time. He told the youth, 'Didn't you hear the young master? How much they give depends on people's kindness.' He turned to Sanjay. 'Isn't that so, sir?'

Sanjay nodded dully. 'People's kindness. Yes, it all depends.'

Collins dismantled the tripod. He strode past the grieving family and pulled his flag off the edge of the shack. The breeze lifted again and the cloth billowed into a bright, gay sail. The photographer battled to fold it. To Sanjay, he looked like an awkward sailor stranded outside his element.

Collins marched off toward the other shacks, muttering to himself. Sanjay smiled awkwardly at the mourning family. The grieving mother still had one hand resting on the chair.

'Is it all right,' she asked, 'if I go inside now?'

Alienation

Samit Basu

Episode 5/5: Sunny Side Up

Sunny was in bed, watching the fan, listening to the rain outside and thinking about how much he hated old, boring, sticky Calcutta, when the phone rang.

For a moment he considered not picking it up, but he was a Dude, and the Dude's Code says: Take The Call, Man. So he got up, pulled on his shorts, stuffed his magazine under the mattress and shuffled out to the hall.

'Hello?'

The voice on the other end was female, and began where sultry left off. It was a voice that picked you off your feet and made you float across the room, like cooking-smell lines in cartoons.

'Iz that Zandeep Zingh?'

Sunny blinked four times as her vocal sub-harmonics ricocheted inside his sixteen-year-old brain. 'Yes,' he said, with some difficulty.

She read out his phone number, and asked him if it was, indeed, his phone number.

'Yes,' said Sunny.

She asked him his address. Sunny, on a roll, said, 'Yes.' After a medium-sized pause, he said, 'Oh,' and then told her his address.

'I'm coming over,' she said. (Yes.)

Sunny did a few quick push-ups. Sunny bathed. Sunny admired himself in the full-length mirror. Sunny combed his hair. Sunny made himself smell nice. Sunny put on smart clothes.

The bell rang.

'Call me Queenie,' said the skimpily clad rain-drenched vision of loveliness that stood outside. She looked even better than she sounded.

'Yes.'

She entered his room. 'You love BuzyBee Burgerz, don't you?'

He considered telling her he thought McDonald's was better, but he was a Smoothie, and the Smoothie's Code says: Go With The Flow, Man. 'Yes.'

'Do you like my body?' she asked, taking off her top.

Resisting the urge to spontaneously explode, he looked. He liked. 'Yes.'

'You may have zex with me now.'

A choir of angels was singing a full-blast aria somewhere, but Sunny was a Good Boy. Says the Code: What The Hell Are You Doing, Man? 'Wait,' said Sunny. 'Who are you? Why are you here?'

'Do you want the zex or not?'

'Yes.'

'Right, then.'

But Sunny was a Twenty-first Century Metrosexual. Code: Protection, Man. 'I don't have protection.'

'That will not be nezezzary,' said Queenie.

Inside his head, Dude, New-Age Man, Good Boy and Smoothie were all yelling No, Man! at Sunny, but there is a Code that trumps all other Codes.

Sunny was a Male Virgin, and the Male Virgin Code says, no, shouts: THIS IS IT, MAN!

They looked at each other, then she stepped forward and kissed him. The moment was perfect. Trees swayed sensuously outside. Lizards watched from the walls. A neighbour helpfully put on a romantic Bhangra remix. From his poster behind the door, Arnie (the Real Man) smiled and jiggled his pectorals approvingly as Queenie went to work.

'Yes,' said Sunny, after a while.

'Yes,' he said again, after a while. And again. And again, and so on.

'You were wonderful,' she smiled afterwards.

'Who are you?' he asked quietly, afraid he would wake up.

'I'm the Queen of the Hive,' she said.

'What's that?'

'Well, we're bazically from another planet,' said Queenie. 'And we're trying to unite, peazefully, with your world. Zo now that you have fertilized me, I can lay my eggz, have millionz of babiez and then die.'

'What?'

'Our babiez will be able to zurvive on both your planet and mine,' she said. 'A new generation of the Hive, bringing our worldz together in the mozt pleazurable way pozzible, yez?'

Sunny stared at her.

'Don't bother your zilly little head with theze detailz,' she said, reaching for him again. 'You'll never zee me again, or have to worry about anything. I juzt thought you should know that you've ensured the zurvival of my people. I'm the only queen and thiz was my only chanze.'

'But. . .'

'I know. Why zpend my only chanze on you of all people? Well, it'z not az random az it zeemz. Do you remember filling in the contezt zection of the feedback form at BuzyBee Burgerz the lazt time you were there?'

Sunny's mouth was full, and he was rapidly losing interest in conversation anyway, but he mumbled and nodded.

'The Hive runz BuzyBee Burgerz all over your world,' continued Queenie, smiling approvingly at his frenzied efforts. 'Our rezearch showed uz thiz waz the bezt way to find a potential drone, whoze DNA ztructures matched the zuitable egg-fertilizer profile – we needed to cut acrozz razez, culturez and zocial groupz, zo mazz-produced genetically modified junk food waz the anzwer. We inzert a zerum in our burgerz that briefly alterz human mental compozition and enablez potential dronez to read the zecret queztion hidden between the linez in the contezt zection of our feedback form.'

'Glub,' said Sunny, some part of his mind registering that relevant information was being imparted.

She patted his head encouragingly. 'You're doing very well,' she said.

'Anyway,' she continued, 'when you ate at Buzybee, our chemical made you zee the real question in the feedback form, which you anzwered correctly. Zo I came to Calcutta, called you and came over to have zex with you, and in a while I'll make my way to the hatching zite. It'z all very zimple, really.'

Sunny looked up. 'Mm,' he said.

'Luckily for you, you were the firzt perzon in the world to anzwer the queztion correctly, zo you got me. There are other people in your world who could have done the job, but I'm glad it waz you – you're zweet, and very energetic, and all our millionz of children will venerate your name az they zlowly rize to power in your world.'

'I'm ready to do it again,' said Sunny.

Luckily for Sunny, Queenie could only lay her eggs after sunset, and so had a few hours to spare. In those few hours, she also told him the history of the Hive, and its plans for the colonization of the galaxy, but Sunny was too occupied making noises like an overworked steam engine to really take in what she said.

Finally, when he was too tired to spawn more inter-planetary hybrid hatchlings, she got up, thanked him, kissed him tenderly and left. So pleased was she at the thought of her happy eggs that she forgot to put her clothes on, which caused Sunny's mother, who'd been outside ringing the doorbell for a very long time, a fair amount of concern.

Sunny lay in bed, watching the fan, listening to the rain and his mother yelling, and thought how much he loved eternal, calm, monsoon-blessed Calcutta.

Damn, he thought, she hadn't left her number. But now he could tell all his friends he'd DONE IT. Of course she'd call back later. He looked at Arnie's poster behind the door, and he could have sworn the Real Man winked.

In a corner of his mind, though, there were a few questions demanding immediate attention from his very tired brain. Had she said she was going to die? Why had she been going on about BuzyBee Burgers? Dudes didn't go there, they went to classy joints like McD. What was all that about aliens? And feedback forms? Who in their right mind filled feedback forms?

Also, should he have let her know that his name was really Sanjay Khanna and that he'd liked her voice so much he couldn't tell her she had the wrong person?

Episode 4/5: Great Balls of Fur
The Antarctic is a cold place.

It's also large, and, except for ice and lost documentary filmmakers, largely empty. It's the Antarctic's largeness and emptiness that make it the perfect continent in which to carry out secret, hideous military experiments. That is, if you don't mind the cold. Universal recognition of this has led to nearly every major power dedicating a spy satellite to watching what every other major power is doing in this vast frozen wasteland. Not very much has been found, but interestingly there's now a huge underground market for dubbed polar-bear pornographic videos in military circles.

Somewhere in this cold, large and empty continent, ignored by these spy satellites, a group of penguins was waddling in circles of consternation around what appeared to be a giant pink furball.

A hatch opened in the furball, and about twenty brightly coloured aliens popped out and bounced around on the ice, whooping loudly and occasionally squashing penguins. These aliens were essentially five-foot spheres of coloured fur, with three bright black button-like ears and five long, thin arms with hands at the ends. Occasionally they would stand on three of these arms and wave their other two around, making sounds like 'Beep!', 'La-La-La!' and sometimes even 'Poogoo-goo!'

Apart from eating fish, looking cute and carrying their children on their feet, penguins don't do much. One of the many things they don't do is watch TV. If they had been TV watchers, or moviegoers, or even cereal eaters, they would have recognized these brightly coloured, bouncing, whooping furball-like aliens for what they were – the stars of the cult children's TV show, *The GlopGlops*.

The GlopGlops were worried. They knew the Toymaker would be furious when they met him. And they had no one to blame – they'd gotten drunk somewhere in the vicinity of Neptune and had gone on a spree that could potentially destroy all the Toymaker's efforts over the last few years, and completely derail the GlopGlop plan to conquer the planet in the bargain. They'd flashed satellites, chased fighter jets, waved at farmers in the American Midwest and given the Sphinx a giant red clown's nose.

Having chased away the last of the penguins, the GlopGlops huddled together like pool balls and had a worried council.

'Eee-ooo!' (The Toymaker should be here any moment now. I'm really worried. He'll be really angry.)

'Gopfiz.' (I'm more sad than angry. We were supposed to be the ship that initiated Phase Three of the takeover process. And we're supposed to be in some place called Tokyo. Instead, we're sitting in the middle of bloody freezing nowhere.)

'Pgoeey-glick!'

'Bogdidi?' (I beg your pardon?)

'Ur-pgofey-glick!' (Sorry, piece of ice in my eye. What I was saying was, look, he's here already.)

The Toymaker's air-chariot arced over a cliff and screeched to a stop a few feet away from the GlopGlops. When the door slid open, the GlopGlops gasped in fear – for sitting next to the Toymaker was the oldest alien on Earth: a suave, handsome, fork-tongued, black-suited man known in Galactic Parliament as the Media Planner. He wore black shades, which, to his extremely hip inner circle, was a huge joke.

The Toymaker slithered out of the chariot and changed into GlopGlop costume.

'Gentlemen!' he said jovially. 'You are a worthless bunch of outer space freaks who should be marooned on a noontime talk show. But you chose a good day to make your mess, because it doesn't matter any more. Phase Three proceeds as planned, but from now on, all your messes will be covered up.'

The Media Planner smiled. 'I've had what is best described as a change of heart, gentlemen,' he said. 'I've decided that Big-Ears' Empire is out of fashion, and the children of this planet need more happiness. Which is why I've decided to sign you up.'

The Toymaker had done very well without the Planner's help, of course. Already, children all over the world were refusing to function if denied their insanely expensive GlopGlop merchandise, be it cereals or underwear. The coffers were overflowing. And with Phase Two – the passing of legislation which enabled humans in GlopGlop costume to lead their entire lives in costume without harassment – the Toymaker had established himself as a force to be reckoned with. What had finally prompted the Planner to break the Parliamentary Accord and team up with the Toymaker was the success of *Balls* – the classic, ironic, hilariously violent and utterly cool movie by iconic filmmaker Ludovic del Aqua, about a gang of anti-imperialist cocaine-addicted free-loving urban terrorists who lived and killed in GlopGlop costumes. *Balls* had turned the GlopGlops from children's toys to mascots for the oppressed overnight, and had signalled the transition to Phase Two of the Toymaker's plan. The Media Planner, who'd casually been spreading alien messages to the people of the world through cartoons, pop music, soap operas, evangelical programmes and home shopping networks for decades, had been impressed by the speed with which the Toymaker established his merchandise distribution networks; how he had grown from a minor player (who merely sought to make action figures of his clients and make these so common that children would be unafraid when the furry aliens actually landed) to a wheeler-dealer running book chains, theme parks, multiplexes and massive advertising campaigns persuading people to live their entire lives walking the streets in GlopGlop costumes. Ultimately, the Toymaker and the Planner found their networks overlapped to such an extent that they either had to work together or fight it out.

The Toymaker's sublime skills (and the fact that Big-Ears, the Imperial representative on Earth, was an annoying moron) had won the Planner over.

'As you know, I've been looking for the perfect brand ambassadors for a while,' said the Planner. 'And I thought that subtly influencing minds the way the Dreamwebbers do is just too much effort. It's all very well, discussing philosophy and making galactic plans – but power is about so much more than intellect.'

'The Media Planner and I have great plans,' said the Toymaker. 'We envisage a future where we can mingle freely with the natives without their even being aware of it – as it is, their simple minds are responding to the GlopGlop cultural overdose by becoming even simpler. As we start Phase Three – the actual mingling with the natives – I urge you caution. We must keep Parliament off our backs until we are ready to move to Phase Four – and so the locals must think you're humans in costume. Your set of instructions about this planet is ready in my chariot.'

The only problem, thought the Planner, as the GlopGlops bounced around, cheering, was the bloody pollen. Wherever they went, GlopGlop fur spread pollen that in unvaccinated planets caused outbreaks of mysterious diseases that killed millions. Epidemic risk, along with extreme culture shock, was one of the principal reasons for the Parliamentary Accord's comprehensive ban on unsupervised landings. But they were working on a cure, and if only the bloody humans stayed home and watched TV all day they'd be safe. . .

'GlopGlop!' cried the GlopGlops as they got into their giant furball and bounced off a little later.

'Plans for this evening?' asked the Media Planner.

'I'm making these new versions of the GlopGlop action figures,' said the Toymaker.

'What's new about them?'

'They carry guns.'

Episode 3/5: Burger Queen

Arindam Sen had a terrible secret. And it wasn't that he was gay – everyone knew *that*. It was something quite different.

He got high on burgers.

'I'll have the Mega Chicken Buzz Burger with fries, please,' he said, each word bubbling glutinously in his throat. He carried his BuzyBee Burger tray back to his table hurriedly, casting sidelong glances around him to make sure no one he knew was there. Arindam Sen, Last of the Intellectuals, stuffing his refined, angst-ridden face at BuzyBee Burgers? He'd never hear the end of it.

But as he opened the flap and held the burger in his hand, he forgot everything else in his lust. His teeth sank into the comforting, synthetic junk, spilling mayonnaise down his kurta. For that brief, glorious instant, everything was forgotten – all the tumultuous anguish, all the poetic world-weariness, and even the perfidy of Orpheus Publishers, who'd tossed his slim volume of poetry aside like a sack of potatoes. Fried potatoes.

Golden, crisp, salty fried potatoes, ululating unsaturated-fattedly from the BuzyBee Burgers carton. He stuffed about seven into his mouth. He couldn't really blame the publishers, though – the market for books of melancholy free-verse poetry about burgers, he had to accept, was limited.

Funny how he'd spent the last few nights dreaming of Vijay, not of burgers – as if someone had flipped a switch inside his head. Mysterious, glamorous Vijay, who drove around in a specially revamped Ambassador, looking like a fashion designer's wet dream. Vijay, who was simply out of his league. Arindam knew he would cry when he went back home in the afternoon to his black-walled room, smoked some grass and re-read some Kafka. But for now, there was the burger.

He bit into it again, and his mind seemed to decompose and coalesce in delirious ecstasy. All around him, ads for burgers, fat, happy families stuffing their faces, and striped waiters merged into a thick, gooey mass of ketchup-flavoured bliss. If only Vijay were here, he thought, life would be perfect.

'Hello, damsel,' said Vijay, materializing out of nowhere and sliding sexily into the seat next to him. 'Enjoying the burger?'

'Whaa. . .' went Arindam, his mind oscillating crazily between happiness and confusion.

Vijay touched his arm, sending ant-columns of hunger-enhanced desire marching down his spine.

'Yes, it's a nutritious burger,' Arindam managed finally, watching everyone in BuzyBee watch Vijay.

'Great,' said Vijay, 'and you do want BuzyBee Burgers to know how much you like their nutritious burgers, don't you?'

'Yes,' said Arindam, a seed of doubt growing in his mind. A sesame seed. On a bun. A nice, soft, warm, happy bun. . .

'Fill in the feedback form,' said Vijay, holding one in front of him.

'Feedback forms? Who fills feedback forms?'

'Do it, damsel. For me.'

'Okay.' Arindam held the BuzyBee Burgers Customer Response Form (Be The Buzz) and tried to focus, because the letters in the contest section kept going for little strolls. But it was pointless.

'I'm sorry, I get high on BuzyBee burgers,' he giggled nervously. 'I can't fill this form.'

'I thought as much,' said Vijay, smiling enigmatically. 'Here, I'll fill it up for you.'

'What do you mean, you thought as much? No one knows my secret.'

'Let's just say I saw you in a dream.'

The letters of the contest question had now settled in completely new positions. Arindam blinked. 'It's a different question,' he told Vijay. 'The question's changed.'

'Answer the question, damsel,' said Vijay, his voice suddenly hoarse.

'Um. . .Queen Bee.'

'Right.'

'So how are you, Vijay?'

'I have to go. I'm dropping this form in the box for you.'

'But you don't know my phone number,' said Arindam feebly.

'Silly damsel,' said Vijay. 'I know everything about you.'

He scribbled a number and a name on Arindam's form and dropped it into the collection box.

As he walked out of Buzybee Burgers, Vijay could hardly suppress his laughter. Trust the Hive to pick a gay man, he thought. Now he didn't even have to kill him. Which was good – he was still uncomfortable about the killing.

He pressed a button on his watch, and his uber-Ambassador roared up to a halt in front of him. 'Let's move,' he said to the hulking chauffeur. 'There are some toys I need to buy.'

Episode 2/5: Minds over Matter

In Camden Town, north London, amidst hundreds of tiny stores selling clothes, music, food, second-hand furniture and mountains of miscellaneous memorabilia, amidst hordes of jostling drug-pushers, lovers, bargain-hunters, criminals, students, plainclothes policemen and tourists, a trio of unusual people made their way towards a costume shop.

There, amidst rows upon rows of grotesque masks and costumes, they huddled together in a corner and spoke in urgent whispers, unnoticed by everyone except the pimpled youth manning the monitor on the hidden security camera. But Stan had been dumped that morning by Audrey, his red-headed main-squeeze from suburban Birmingham, and so failed to notice that the Dreamwebber seemed to blur a little every time she moved, that the Toymaker left a faint trail of dust behind him and that the Media Planner's feet never actually touched the ground. Of course, no camera captured the Planner's vaguely sulphurous smell, so Stan could not be blamed for that.

The aliens hadn't been so lucky on their way to Camden Market from the Tube station, though. A Turkish speed addict named Kerimoglu – loaded to the gills with methamphetamines freshly smuggled from the Golden Triangle by a crazed Dane named Ulrik – had seen them and started screaming and clutching his much-pierced face. His fellow punks were British, though, and had merely tut-tutted sadly as they watched him having a fit. One, a neo-Visigoth named Julian, had coughed self-deprecatingly and whispered 'Bloody Turk' to his leather-clad love-slave Keith, who'd nodded.

'We don't have much time,' said the Toymaker. 'Imperial agents are close by.'

'I wonder how they knew we were here,' said the Dreamwebber, looking sharply at the Planner.

'I have nothing to do with it,' lied the Media Planner. 'Anyway, we don't have much time, so let's get straight to business.'

'The Hive is up to its old tricks,' said the Toymaker. 'This time, they're looking for drones through a fast-food chain. They've inserted this serum. . .'

'I think we've all heard about that; it's not exactly been subtle,' said the Dreamwebber. 'At least, I have, and I've already sent someone to deal with it.'

The others looked at her in surprise.

'Since when have the Dreamwebbers started physically intervening in Earth affairs?' asked the Planner.

'We don't intervene, Azrael,' she replied sharply. 'We remain committed to our ideals. But the Hive has broken the Accord yet again. And every day we waste deliberating will increase the chances of millions of Hive eggs being laid in some remote location on this planet. We acted now simply because we don't have the resources to start a planet-wide search later.'

'But how did you find out, Denise?' asked the Toymaker.

'The usual way. There were huge slashes in the fabric of the dream-web. The serum they use causes potential drones to dream of eating junk food. Of course, quite a few natives do that without chemical assistance – it's incredible how primitive they are.'

'Not primitive, Denise – innocent. That's why we're here, aren't we?'

'I'm impressed that you'll take physical action, though,' said the Planner. 'I wonder what Big-Ears will say when he gets to hear of it. Maybe the Empire will desire an alliance with the Dreamwebbers, if their methods converge.'

'The Dreamwebbers remain committed to the Accord,' she replied firmly. 'Brute force is beneath us. This is a special case, and you know it. It's just that my assassin is, strangely enough, from the same city as the drone we've identified. Must be something in the air that makes them receptive.'

Two Imperial troopers, dressed as Japanese tourists (the ineffective disguise they used all over the world), marched into the store.

'Big-Ears' boys are here again,' said the Toymaker indulgently. 'I think it's really impressive the way he's managed to make the global media sell his lies, though.'

'He's harming the planet irreparably,' said the Dreamwebber, as the troopers, having taken a few photographs, left. 'The usual throw-planet-into-confusion-before-invasion-by-making-up-stupid-excuse-for-random-war method has worked well, but the natives here don't know when to stop. When the Empire gets here, there won't be much left. Unless we negotiate the terms of colonization between ourselves, and prepare some kind of common defence before the Empire gets here.'

'The Empire is already here, my friends,' said the Media Planner. 'Get used to it.'

He looked at his diamond-encrusted watch. 'I have to go now,' he said suavely. 'We should do lunch sometime. Vegas.'

'He's in league with Big-Ears,' said the Dreamwebber, as she watched him brush by an elderly couple in matching King Kong costumes on his way out.

'I know,' replied the Toymaker. 'But he'll be taken care off. Parliament is not stupid, you know.'

We're all looking for ways to stab each other in the back, he thought. But at least we do it in a civilized manner.

Episode 1/5: Operation Vijay

'I'll get to the point,' she said. I could have stared at her beautiful green eyes for hours without complaining, but I nodded earnestly at her. This is America, I thought. They get to the point here.

A month ago

Dear Vijay,
Congratulations!
Your story, SpiderDream, has won the Global Short SF-Fantasy Story Contest organized by
www.thewebofdreams.com
As promised, we're going to fly you to New York and give you the job you've always dreamed of!

Three days ago

'I'm going to New York, Mother.'

'Heh?'

'New York! The story I wrote in a day? The online writing contest I won, remember? The prize?'

'Heh?'

'Look at me! I'm. . .going. . .to. . .New. . .York.'

'Will you be home for dinner?'

Fifteen minutes ago

'Vijay? Very glad to finally meet you. I'm Denise Nebula, the editor.'

I stared at the stunning twenty-something woman in front of me, trying to keep my jaw from dropping. I thought people associated with science fiction were all slightly overweight, dishevelled, spaced-out, a little nerdy even.

People like me.

But Ms Nebula (Please, call me Denise) looked like she'd just come back from a *Cosmopolitan* shoot. The legs, the hair, the face, the. . .

Anyway.

I followed her like a little lamb to her plush office and we sat.

'Please tell me all about yourself.'

So I did.

Three seconds ago

'I'll get to the point.'

I think that brings me more or less up to date.

Denise leaned forward.

'I'm not from this planet,' she said.

'What?'

'Don't look so alarmed. I – we – mean you no harm. In fact, I have great news for you.'

Beautiful woman who thinks she's an alien? I can deal with that, I thought. All Americans are crazy, anyway. Well-known fact.

'The reason we organized this contest,' she said, 'was to find the earthling whose vision of extraterrestrials corresponded most closely to our reality. Your DreamSpiders, Vijay, are just like us Dreamwebbers – a race of peaceful beings of superior intellect.'

I smiled at her. She's mad, I thought, but at least she's harmless.

'So your website is actually run by aliens,' I grinned. 'Studying earthlings, no doubt.'

'Yes,' she said, smiling in turn, 'I'm glad you understand. The creativity implant worked particularly well with you, I see.'

'The what?'

'This is going to shock you a little, Vijay.'

'I think I can handle it.'

'There are a number of extraterrestrial races already present on earth, all engaged in a race to establish contact first. We could conquer your world easily, of course, but the Parliament forbids it.'

'So you use science fiction as a peaceful alternative means of contact?'

'Yes. Science fiction is not a human invention, but a result of certain signals we send out – brain images commonly called dreams.'

I was beginning to feel a little scared. The whole SpiderDream idea had come to me in a dream.

'This sci-fi contest had only one purpose, Vijay – to find an ambassador. We need a human ambassador to execute our policies on Earth – we Dreamwebbers prefer to confine ourselves to the intellectual plane unless strictly necessary.'

'Wait a minute,' I said. 'You mean that science fiction is what aliens tell us about themselves in our dreams?'

'Yes. To be brutally frank, you humans are simply not capable of thinking beyond politics, sex and violence on your own. It's not your fault – you simply aren't evolved enough. Science fiction – and fantasy – are the Dreamwebbers' ways of helping you. Gentle pushes towards evolution, delivered as you walk the web of dreams.'

'And that's the job you're offering me? To be your ambassador?'

'Yes, Vijay. Picture it. Interstellar travel, money, worlds beyond your imagination,' she leaned forward further and smiled even more seductively. 'And there are other benefits. . .'

'There's a slight problem,' I said.

'What is it?'

'I don't believe you.'

'I knew it wouldn't be easy,' she sighed. 'But I have proof. Have you read *Lord of the Rings*?'

'Of course. Twelve times.'

She sighed again, like someone trying to explain something to an idiot child.

'Do you seriously think Tolkien was human?'

The office seemed to spin around me. I suddenly realized that she was telling the truth. . .

'You're telling me the truth, aren't you.'

'As promised, the job you've always dreamed of,' she said.

What could I say? It was an offer I couldn't refuse. Who would?

But there was one question. One all-important question. Because, after all, this concerned the whole planet, the future of the human race. . .

'How much do I get paid?'

She mentioned a sum. It was enough.

'When can I start?'

'Today! But first, just sign the contract.'

A typed sheet of paper appeared in front of me. I read it carefully.

Nothing wrong with it. I signed the contract.

'What happens now? Press conferences? Space travel? An advance payment? What?'

Why not go for broke, I thought.

'Or maybe we could discuss all this somewhere more private?'

'This meeting is over, Vijay,' smiled Denise. 'We'll start the preparation for the opening of the embassy immediately, if you don't mind.'

She pressed a button on her desk. 'The Beautician is on his way,' she said.

'So I get a makeover? The pimples removed, and so on?'

'No, Vijay. One thing we have come to realize is that your planet values good looks above anything else. Which is why

I, for example, got this body made for me. The Beautician will construct an entirely new body – the ambassador must be the most handsome man on the planet.'

The door opened behind me. Something very large entered the room.

'I'm afraid your body doesn't meet the requirements, Vijay,' smiled Denise.

'What does that mean?' I asked.

'That means, Vijay,' she said, 'that we'll just take your brain.'

Ajji's Miracle

Anita Rau Badami

THESE DAYS THE OLD WOMAN, AJJI, HOBBLES AROUND THE house so full of herself that if you poke her with a pin she might explode. She shouts orders, bullies the servants, eats enormous meals and then farts painfully through the night. She makes such a racket screaming, 'Amma, Amma, Ammamma!' before every resounding expulsion of gas, that nobody else can sleep. Her daughter-in-law Rukku, who was the queen of the house just a few months ago, can only watch sullenly, her mind full of vicious thoughts against Ajji. Sometimes she finds it difficult to believe the way things have been turned upside down in her own home. As for poor young Tara, she can do nothing but pout and cry a little and wait for Ajji's miracle to occur. After all, if it had not been for her, Ajji would still have been sitting in a corner of the house like a pile of old clothes, begging her grandchildren for love or, if not that, at least a piece of jaggery.

*

This is how it all changed.

There was a time when Ajji used to sit quietly in the verandah, peering at a religious book or staring out at the road. At twelve o'clock she would summon her younger grandchild, a boy of six, and say, 'Go and tell your mother that you can hear Ajji's stomach grumbling. Go, go, my putta, my sweet lump of sugar.'

She was too scared to approach Rukku herself. Who knew, if she was in a bad mood, she might make Ajji wait till two o'clock for her lunch. But the little boy now, he was different. He was his mother's pet, anything he said was law. Quite different from her attitude toward her daughter Tara. This caused a lot of friction in the house, naturally, for Tara was Ajji's favourite. She was the one who stole little bits of bella for Ajji when the old woman was overcome with a craving for something sweet, and it was she who always listened patiently to Ajji's rambling stories of gods and goddesses.

'Oh Ajji,' the dear child would say, 'tell me again about Lord Krishna and the snake,' or, 'Ajji, my favourite Ajji, tell me the one about Lord Ganesha and the moon.'

In this lonely world full of loud-mouthed daughters-in-law and limp-as-pyjama sons, Tara's attentions made Ajji feel like she still existed. Toothless and fleshless Ajji was, but not a corpse yet. Oh yes, she still had her wits about her! And all her jewellery, without which Ajji might not have been able to maintain her precarious position in this household. She thanked her good sense often for having held on to her gold chains and rings and diamond earrings and nose-studs, her bangles and armbands. When her son Kitta was newly married, she had been tempted to give her chains and earrings to Rukku, so pretty and innocent she had looked. Lurking under that charming exterior, however, was a screeching rakshasi. Oh yes, how she had simpered and smiled and worn those tight little blouses. How she had wrapped her husband's eyes with ribbons of desire, until Kitta was so drunk on her body juices that he willingly turned over every penny that he earned to her. Not his mother, mind, not like he used to, and with that pay packet, with that little slip of a cheque, slid Ajji's power in the house that her husband had built. In the blink of an eyelash Rukku had usurped her throne, had become maharani, the whip, Queen of England. Within a month of her arrival, she had kicked Ajji out of her room into the smallest chamber with one little window high in the wall, right next to the noisy street. In front of Kitta though, Rukku behaved like a respectful daughter-in-law, but as soon as the fool left for work, she was transformed. No use complaining to the besotted fool either. Yes, Ajji admitted that her only son was an idiot, men never did understand the currents that ran through a household full of women. Only knew how to shift from one pair of breasts to another. That's all, that's all, hunh! Ajji cursed her own dead husband for leaving her in the shadow of her son's cowardly frame, for leaving her to tolerate Rukku's tyrannies.

The old woman had her own ways of taking revenge though. Guerrilla style she would launch sneak attacks and then retreat to her corner to sit there innocent as an empty sky. Rukku's favourite sari would develop a sudden tear, one of her slippers might disappear, the screw of her gold earring would get lost, forcing her to spend for a replacement. Ajji's favourite act of vengeance was to go to the neighbours' homes and ask for food. 'I should have died long ago,' she would say, wiping her eyes with the end of her sari. 'I don't know what my past sins are that this body still exists. How much trouble it causes everybody, I can't bear to think about it.'

At this point the neighbour might say kindly, 'Come now Ajji, why are you so bitter today?'

And Ajji, wiping the wet off the end of her nose would reply, 'Ah what can I say? I don't want to be accused of eating the salt from a house and then cursing it. Though, to be honest, that is all I get to eat these days you know, just salt and a bit of rice. Oh my sinful past, to have reduced me to this sorry state! Oh, oh, oh!'

The neighbour would pat Ajji on her shoulder and say, 'It's all right Ajji. Why don't you come inside and eat something, you do look like you haven't eaten all day, poor thing.'

And Ajji again, hiding her triumph, 'I can't lie, may god bite my tongue if I do, I can't lie and say that I have eaten. But then she is my daughter-in-law after all, I chose her myself from a line-up long as this road for my son, so I must bear my sorrow in my own belly.'

The old woman went to a different house each day. That way all the neighbours knew that Rukku was ill-treating her mother-in-law and, even better, Ajji got to taste so many different types of cooking – the rasam in the house next door was wonderful, the govardhan-kai palya in that one there was amazing, and nothing to beat the rich taste of puliyodarey from that one across the road.

When the girl Tara was born Rukku cried with disappointment at not having had a male child. But Ajji, lamenting her own fate in bearing only one son (who had turned into his wife's tail), immediately declared that her diamond earrings and three of the fat gold chains strung about her parchment neck would go to Tara when she was married. 'Of course,' she added, 'it all depends on whose side of the family she takes after. I covered my daughter-in-law with gold when she stepped into this house and see where that has left me!'

Rukku could do nothing more than curse mentally and say in her most ingratiating voice, 'As it is I am wretched, instead of an heir for my husband I have produced a burden. Without your help how can we manage?' She gave Ajji a sweet smile and added, 'See the girl looks just like you. Promises to be a beauty!'

'Her eyes are like a pair of lotuses,' agreed Ajji. 'And her nose like the stem of a jasmine. I'll have to rub it with almond oil every day to keep it that way, like my own grandmother did for me you know.' The next day when she did her lunchtime rounds of the neighbours' homes, Ajji said with a sigh, 'Thank the lord Krishna she did not take after her mother. A nose like a cauliflower would have been her fate.'

If the girl grew up the way Ajji wanted her to, the old woman reflected after the day was done, she would get a pair of diamond earrings. They were Ajji's most precious possessions, so heavy that they had pulled the holes of her earlobes out of shape and now hung on a thin slice of brown skin. Ajji had seen Rukku eyeing those earrings. Let her hunger for them, she thought, she isn't going to get them anyway. But by promising them alternately to Rukku and to Tara, Ajji knew that she could wring a fairly decent life for herself in this house. Yes, it was a good thing that a girl-child had crawled out of Rukku's womb.

When the boy-child was born, Tara receded even further in her mother's affections. She became a ghostly being who might have faded into nothingness if it had not been for Ajji's exuberant attentions. It was Ajji who sang to Tara when she was a baby, revelling in the sound of her own voice from which music had fled many years ago. 'Jo-jo, laali mari, may sugar sprinkle your dreams, tender pink lilies touch you to sleep,' she carolled, rocking and soothing and petting little Tara to sleep.

Every Sunday the grandmother massaged the girl's thin body with oil before giving her a hot bath. 'Now that will make your arms flow like lotus stems,' Ajji would say, kneading and slapping Tara's arms in the hot sun of the courtyard. 'And that will make your face smoother than honey.'

While Tara grumbled and cried as the sharp mustard oil stung her skin, and Rukku from inside the house yelled to the world that the old witch was giving the child an inflated sense of her importance, Ajji's hands coaxed lustre out of her grandchild's skin.

'Lucky for you your old granny is still alive to look after you,' she said, twisting and wringing Tara's arms, grunting as she rubbed her back. 'That mother of yours doesn't care. She is only waiting for the day some man will come for you, that's all. But I, I won't let you go anywhere my pet, I will always be here for you.' She would wait expectantly, her hands stilled and then smile when Tara said sulkily, 'And I will always be here for you my darling Ajji.'

It was as if Tara's existence lent power to the old woman. So what if Rukku screamed and complained? As long as the girl was there, Ajji had a little corner in the house. The ritual continued even when the girl turned sixteen, grown taller, but still as slim as a bamboo shoot.

So it was that Ajji was the first to notice that Tara's breasts were developing unevenly. While the right one had attained the right size, the left remained flat. At first Ajji kept quiet about it, rubbing oil onto Tara's chest even harder, hoping to stimulate the force that lay beneath the skin and made breasts grow. When coconut oil proved ineffective, she spent her own money and bought castor oil, hoping the denser fluid would work better. Nothing at all. Ajji hobbled to the ayurvedic doctor down the street. She trusted him far more than she did the posh new fellows with modern ideas and foreign degrees who made you pay through your nose, cut off a part of your body and then sold it to somebody else for a fortune. Yes, yes, Ajji had heard all about those big hospitals and the things that went on in there. Why just yesterday, the temple priest's sister was telling her about her aunt's grandson who went to the hospital with a sore throat. Only a sore throat, see? But he made a mistake going to a big-shot hospital. The priest told him not to but who listened to their elders these days? The smart suit doctor sent the boy to another doctor who sent him somewhere else and before he could say aan or oon, they had him on an operating table. Took out his appendix, they said, but who knows what else they pulled out? The boy had been married six years now and still his wife's belly remained flat! Worse, who knew what they had put in? These foreign-trained doctors did all sorts of inauspicious things, put monkeys' hearts in humans, pigs' kidneys, dogs' eye-balls anything they could lay their hands on!

Ajji came away from the doctor bearing a large jar of malam from Singapore. The doctor had assured her that it contained nothing but the best herbs and berries, ancient ones that did not grow in India anymore.

For the next few weeks Ajji religiously massaged Tara's chest with the ointment. She also forced the girl to eat large balls of fresh butter – perhaps, she thought, the child was not getting enough fatty foods. The jar of malam was almost empty and Tara's left breast remained indifferent to the attention.

It was time, Ajji felt, that Rukku be alerted to the problem. 'I don't want to try anything else,' she reflected. 'Then if something happens, all the blame will be on my head. No, I will tell that stupid woman, Tara is her daughter after all.'

She went on the offensive right away. 'Enh Rukku, do you know anything that is going on in this house? Your own daughter, that too? If my eyes, old but still good, hadn't noticed, god only knows what would have happened!'

'What? What is it?' demanded Rukku, her mind racing over all the things that could have happened to a girl. 'Is it the pimply boy in Number 65? I have told that wretched Tara not to go by that house. So many different roads to school and still she will go that way only. That loafer sits there ogling girls all day. What has he done to Tara?'

'If your daughter was like you then you would have to worry,' replied Ajji in a sly voice.

'What do you mean, you evil old gossip? Eat my food and spread rumours about me!' Rukku screamed.

'You think these old eyes haven't seen what goes on in this house? You think I haven't seen how you talk to that cousin of yours? Oh my, he is like a brother you said, oh my! But leave all that for now, perhaps he is like your brother, my eyes might be worse than I thought. Let us worry about your daughter now.'

'Enh old woman, you want to lose your corner in this house?' Rukku said, fiercely tucking the end of her sari pallu into her waistband. 'Maybe you want to take your gold chains and earrings and all and buy a room somewhere else, enh?'

Ajji sucked in her teeth and filled her eyes with tears. 'How quickly you get angry my dear. Didn't I say that my eyes were bad? I am an old woman, sometimes my tongue gets jumbled up and then, who knows what not falls out. Eh, all I worry about is your daughter.'

Rukku was silent although she ached to hear what the problem was.

'Maybe you can try on my red-stone bangles this Deepavali,' bargained Ajji. 'Of course that will be possible only if I am still in the house.'

'Ajji, you are like my own mother,' Rukku said, already thinking of a sari to match the bangles. 'I know that you have our welfare at heart always. Now tell me what is wrong with Tara.'

They would start with prayer, they decided, the two of them, Rukku and Ajji. Over the next couple of weeks they covered all the temples in the city. For good measure they appealed to the Muslim and Christian gods as well. God was god, so what did it matter? They went to the big mosque in Fathima Bazaar and tied little wish threads onto pillars that were already covered with thousands of coloured ribbons and paper messages, all addressed to Allah the merciful.

Ajji was a bit doubtful about this method. 'Suppose the Muslim god finds it difficult to read Tamil?' she asked.

'No, no,' assured a woman next to her. 'The almighty one is wise in the language of all beings.'

Another day they pushed through the throngs into the Basilica of Mary and Jesus. That was Rukku's idea. Every day in the papers she had seen messages from the devoted thanking the infant Jesus for a variety of favours granted. At the gates of the basilica, Ajji and Rukku bought a tin cutout of a female torso to deposit in the prayer box along with money. Cutouts of various parts of the body were available here. If you were lame you bought a foot or a whole leg. There were eyes, noses, ears, heads. This god, Ajji thought, was just like Lord Venkateshwara in Tirupathi – words were not enough to tell him about your problems!

'But how will this baby god know which breast isn't growing?' she asked, ever alive to the various misinterpretations even a god could put on earthly messages.

Rukku solved the problem by marking off the afflicted breast with a dab of kumkum liquid that she carried in her purse. It wasn't indelible, but Rukku had faith that the mark would stay long enough for the infant Jesus to see it. Besides, wasn't god omniscient?

A whole month went by and the two women noticed no change in Tara's anatomy. Rukku decided that it was time to tell her husband about this family crisis.

'What can I do?' he demanded irritably. 'This is a woman's matter. What do I know about all this? I am a busy man, so much work in the office and then I have to come home to solve your problems too?'

'Is she my daughter only?' demanded Rukku. 'Did I produce her like Kunthi? Simply held out my arms to the sun and said give me a child and a child I got?'

'Okay, okay,' said her husband, defeated by the noise that Rukku was creating. 'I will ask the company doctor and see what happens.'

The doctor had so many suggestions that Rukku's husband came home with his head abuzz with strange medical terms and a worried feeling that a lot of money was involved. He also got the name of a specialist in the field, who was, as the company doctor put it, 'world famous in all of South India for his thorough knowledge of the subject.'

Ajji insisted on accompanying the family to the specialist's office despite her fear of doctors. She was certain that if he was a fraud, she would be able to spot him straightaway.

The specialist examined Tara and said that the only option was surgery. A Silastic percutaneous tissue-expander would be inserted. This object with a pompous name was only available abroad. Rukku's husband said that they would think things over and hustled his family out.

'See?' Ajji said triumphantly. 'He wants to put rubber bands inside my child's body. I told you these modern fellows are no good. But who wants to listen to me?'

Tara started to weep noisily. Her life appeared to have been reduced to two consuming problems – the breast and how to get her married before the world noticed its absence. Nobody tried to comfort her. Rukku was busy thinking of inexpensive solutions, and Ajji, excited by the smell of problems and conflict, wondered if she could ask the taxi to stop at Grand Sweets for a moment. The thought of their fresh sugar-soaked janghris made her stomach yearn.

'Only abroad you can get this elastic thing,' Rukku said thoughtfully. 'I will write to my cousin Rama. He will surely help. After all, my grandfather was the one who set his grandfather up in business. So their family fortunes are really due to the goodness of my grandfather.'

*

Cousin Ramu replied almost immediately from New York. He offered his sympathies but was noncommittal about sending the tissue-expander. It was a product that had been banned in the US, he said, due to possible side effects. And if he did manage to procure one, there was the added complication of cost. A tissue-expander was expensive, and although Cousin Ramu would be only too happy to bear the cost for his beloved cousin, he didn't think it was a good idea to endanger her daughter's health with the product.

Rukku was disappointed with the letter. She had expected her cousin to mail the tissue-expander by return mail. It also gave Ajji the chance to snipe about Rukku's family. 'Now if it was my cousin,' the old woman remarked complacently, 'he would have sent the elastic immediately. But of course only the blessed have such families.'

'So what do we do now?' Rukku asked, ignoring Ajji's comments. 'Not only do I have a daughter-headache, but a daughter with a problem.'

'Don't worry, I will go on a fast,' Ajji declared impulsively. 'Such a strong fast it will be, I tell you, the very heavens will shake. The only things that I will eat are fruit and popcorn.'

'What kind of fast is that?' Rukku asked. 'For a strong fast you should not even touch water.'

'I am too old for that,' said Ajji. 'The gods will understand that I am doing the best that I can. Even Gandhiji ate bananas when he was fasting and he got independence for the country.'

Ajji hadn't planned to fast for more than a week. She thought that her son would decide on an operation before the week ran out. But Kitta was not willing to spend the money yet.

'So what are we going to do?' demanded Ajji, whose stomach was making urgent demands for spicy sambhar, jackfruit-seed curry and lemon rice. This fast business did not agree with her at all.

'I will break a few more coconuts at the Venkateshwara temple and you keep your fast. God will surely listen to two helpless women,' Rukku said.

Ajji grumbled under her breath and included potato chips fried in ghee, sago uppuma, and ice cream in her list of foods that could be eaten during a fast. She told all her neighbours about the fast and the sacrifices that she was making for her granddaughter. Now that everybody on the street knew about the missing breast, poor Tara couldn't leave the house without somebody asking about it. She stopped going out altogether.

'Why did you tell everybody?' she raged at Ajji, who merely patted her on the head and went out to meet a neighbour. Life was finally becoming more interesting than it had been all these barren years and Ajji was not about to let Tara's wounded feelings get in the way of her own enjoyment.

The neighbour had brought some guava jelly for Ajji. 'I know you are fasting, Ajji,' the neighbour said. 'But you can keep this and have it later.'

'Oh but this is fruit after all,' Ajji said. 'It is allowed.'

The neighbour, puffed up with the idea of having a major fast like this happening right next door, told everybody she knew about Ajji. 'Her determination is as terrible as Parvati-devi's,' she said, carried away somewhat. 'Sometimes when she is totally immersed, I can even feel the ground shudder!'

Drawn by the spectacle of a girl without a breast, people from other streets stopped by to see Tara and ended up touching

Ajji's feet. The old woman thrived on the fruit and ice cream that she ate every day even though it upset her digestion a bit. She loved all the attention, even though the original aim of it all was Tara, who refused to show her face outside her room. She demanded fresh lime juice every afternoon and insisted that Rukku squeeze it herself.

'What is the need for all this drama?' Rukku wanted to know, goaded beyond endurance.

'Drama? I am only doing this for your daughter. Now that everybody in the city knows about her problem, only a miracle can find her a groom.' She turned tragic eyes upon her audience of neighbours who had started trickling in. 'After all this penance I am doing my ancient body needs a little sugar. But if my daughter-in-law cannot afford this small indulgence then I will do without it. What is the worst that will happen? I will die of thirst that is all.'

Naturally one of her neighbours offered to bring her a jug of lime juice every day and Rukku could only grind her teeth and yell at the servant maid. She was bitter about this turn of events. She still had Kitta's pay packets but the power in the home had shifted to Ajji. Wasn't the old witch supposed to be fasting for the sake of her granddaughter? Everybody appeared to have forgotten this small fact. A month had gone by since that visit to the doctor, Tara's breast remained flat, but Ajji's eyes sparkled with all the food that she was eating. Yesterday it was potatoes roasted in ghee, today she said that Lord Shiva had appeared to her in a dream and ordered her to eat puli-shaadam on his behalf.

Well, thought Rukku, the old woman had better enjoy this state of affairs. It would surely not last very much longer. Once Tara was tied to some man, things would swing back to normal here. Now with Ajji's growing fame the family prestige had gone up several notches. They were getting offers for the girl's hand. To be connected by marriage to a divinely inspired grandmother was considered an advantage. Perhaps, thought Rukku, they would settle on that boy from the Parthasarathy family. How did it matter if he was so much older than Tara? Till the marriage though, Rukku would have to tolerate Ajji with her ordering and her pretending and her heckling, her eating and farting through the night. But Rukku could wait. She had the patience of a vulture.

In the verandah, Ajji shut her eyes and rocked happily. Her brain clicked busily. She wondered how she could prevent the match from the Parthasarathy family. She couldn't say anything about the horoscopes, she didn't even know which end of it was the right way up. But perhaps she could find an inauspicious mole or twitch on the boy's face and play it up. Tara could wait a bit to get married, Ajji had never had such a good time in her life. Who could have imagined the turn that her old and hitherto miserable life had taken? Truly it was a miracle.

Bollox

Farrukh Dhondy

From: **Gajan69@rediffmail.com**

Dear Mister Crookshag,

Forgive me for intruding like this. It is about your most fortunate find of my cousin who is to donate his part to you through the Wholebody organization. May God bless the transfer. Of course we know that we are not suppose to get in touch with you, but I am doing so for a very particular and religious purpose.

My cousin was definitely told when he signed the papers for Wholebody that he would have no contact with the receiver of his parts. The match for everything, tissue and all this would be done anonymously and the donor and receiver would never know who is whom. We know why it is best this way as there can be no questions asked afterwards. We are still wanting everything to be done through Wholebody itself, but there are some facts which I feel are tending to cause my cousin to withdraw his offer and they are to do with our spiritual beliefs.

I must put it plainly, Mr Crookshag. In our religion we would not mind if the kidney or the heart were donated to someone who is a stranger, but in the particular part that your unfortunate accident demands for transplant is the seat of all energy and procreation according to our holy shastras and power passes from it down from one generation to another. It is the seat of shakti, producing the juice of life and all our sect and my family are feeling that we must know to whom this instrument of vital life-giving source is passing. In whose body will the life-making organ of my cousin come to rest.

You must be knowing the idea of spirit and power passing from one body to another, like Buddhists believe in spirits living in different people through ages. We are not Buddhists but orthodox Hindus with Tantric tradition deep in our family past and though nobody in the family has ever donated a testicle to someone else's body before, we have taken saintly advice and know that it is like passing on life power to another person.

Naturally we want to know that this life power is passed on for good and we are

confident that Wholebody has only found good and deserving people for receivership.
I would request you only that we may know something about you before my cousin can travel to Dubai for the operation. I hope this is not taking you too much by surprise and wish for speedy conclusion of your unfortunate state of affairs.
Your friend
Gajan Nath

From **PROJECTFINANCE@hotmail.com**
Dear Mr Nath,
How did you find my official e-mail address and my name? By the way it is spelt Cruikshank and not as you addressed me in your last. I take this breach of security very seriously and will sue the company for betraying the anonymity I was assured of in the contract and, I may tell you, have paid a considerable sum for?
Yours etc.
Cru.

From: **Gajan69@rediffmail.com**
Dear Mr Cruikashokh,
Sorry for misguiding your name. I will tell the secret. We paid the Mumbai doctor who was hired to carry out the tests on my cousin for blood and tissue type to get in touch with the private clinic in London and find out who the potential receiver of our testicle was going to be. He charged us a

lot of money for finding out. He assured us that my cousin's types in blood and tissue and peculiar things about his DNA are very distinct and rare and so it is God's miracle that they have suited and matched yours and I know it is the hand of Bhagwan that has brought my cousin to your salvation. His testicles are tried and tested as he has three children. Three more were also there but they died of typhoid fever and two of TB. You seem a very good, proud gentleman, determined about the spelling of your name and everything. As I said we would still be reluctant to go through all this without knowing to whom we were giving the life force.

Your friend

Gajan Nath

From **PROJECTFINANCE@hotmail**

Dear Mr Nath,

I appreciate the ideas and sentiment that your religious tradition imposes on you. Oh dear! How am I to say that I am a worthy receiver of the life force. Let me just say that I am to marry for the second time and the young lady to whom I am engaged, though of contemporary thinking in every other way, has not reconciled herself to the fact that we may not have a natural child.

I don't know if you know my circumstances, but owing to an unfortunate accident at first and then a hereditary growth I have had amputations of the organs in question. Though the operation is very rare, the specialist from whom I sought treatment is sure that the transplant will restore my ability to naturally procreate. I have been waiting for years for the correct medical and scientific match to be found and both my fiancée and I were delighted that one had been.

Your communication came out of the blue. Yes, of course we shall respect your sentiments and shall answer any questions you would like to put.

Ever

Cru.

From: **Gajan69@rediffmail.com**
Dear Mr Crookedshark,
Thank you very much for your reply agreeing to answer all questions. May I put to you the circumstance that we are very poor in our family? In fact I am the only earning member and supporting my cousin and family also now. To defray the cost of bribery to the UK clinic to send on papers and the greed of the Mumbai doctor, can you please help with sending me directly three hundred pounds sterling. This will cover everything. I know you will not refuse.

Your friend

Gajan Nath

From **PROJECTFINANCE@hotmail**
Dear Mr Nott,
Believe me I have paid in advance and will
still be paying a considerable sum of money
to Wholebody transactions and have budgeted
myself for the operation and the recovery
etc. Your demand, while entirely reasonable,
must be the last. How shall I send the
money? And after that is done can we proceed
to inform Wholebody without any reference to
this correspondence that your cousin is
ready for the operation.
May I ask one question? If two of your
nephews or nieces died of TB, is there any
vestige of it in the family. Has your
cousin, whose name you haven't told me, ever
suffered from the disease and, if he has,
in which part of his body?
Ever
Cru.

From: **Gajan69@rediffmail.com**
Dear Master Cruukskunk,
Don't send money. A broker of such affairs
will come and fetch it from your office if
you will supply the address by next e-mail.
As for the TB, yes my cousin did have TB
but in his lungs and it was treated
successfully thence you are getting a clear
certificate of health from Wholebody.
Please tell us what your professional and
religious leanings are.
Your friend
Gajan Nath

From **PROJECTFINANCE@hotmail**
The address from which your agent can pick up the cash is 37 De Lancey Close SE 21 3HB. If he can call after office hours it would be most convenient.
I work in the City in a brokerage firm and my religion I suppose is Christian Anglican though I would not call myself devout. I am a believer and probably believe with Mahatma Gandhi that all religions converge in a belief in God. Is that not what he said? I have got a book on Tantric belief out of the library and shall make it my study immediately. I hope these answers are satisfactory. Can we now progress to fix dates?
Ever
Cru.

From: **Gajan69@rediffmail.com**
Dear Mr Crutchshake,
You seem a very diligent person and myself and my cousin are well pleased with your attempt at finding out our religion.
I must mention that the most expeditious way for my cousin to be brought to the same medical centre in the world as yourself to donate his part is for him now to travel to Delhi and file application for a passport which he never anticipated. Wholebody never told him nothing about this arrangements and left it up to individual.
I have to sadly add that this trip and transaction to New Delhi, including bribes

to expedite procedure of passport issue, will cost a small sum of money. Very large to us but proportional to your wants, I believe. It will be about £1700 more Sterling. Without this money we can ask Wholebody to put up costs but I fear they will be refusing. As soon as money reaches through the same channel we will be in swift transit to Delhi. I will have to go myself as my cousin is a simple person and don't know much bureaucracy.
Your good friend
Gajan

From **PROJECTFINANCE@hotmail**
Dear Gajan,
I do understand that a passport is necessary, as I have declined to have the operation in India. I have engaged the best surgeon in a reputable and hygienic clinic which will assure success and will be best for your cousin too.
This last time I feel compelled to send the money.
Etc.
Cru.

From: **Gajan69@rediffmail.com**
Dear Mr Crookshark,
Very pleased to have the cash which arrived safely for which we thank you heartily. What is your star sign, even in western astrology terms?
Your loving friend
Gajan

From **PROJECTFINANCE@hotmail**
Dear Gajan,
I don't understand what my star sign has to do with anything. I have paid you considerable sums now and want you to inform me when your cousin will be ready to travel.
Etc.
Cru.

From: **Gajan69@rediffmail.com**
Dear Crookshaonk,
You are making devious mistake. Pl'ease forward star sign. My cousin is nervous.
Your best friend
Gajan

From **PROJECTFINANCE@hotmail**
Gajan,
It's Taurus.
Cru.

From **PROJECTFINANCE@hotmail**
Gajan,
No word from you. Inform me as to whether the passport has been obtained.
Yours truly
Cru.

From: **Gajan69@rediffmail.com**
Dear Mr Crutchneck,
This is a very terrible situation. I have not disclosed what your star sign is to my cousin but I know a very bad fact. My cousin

is a superstitious fellow, which I am not dear sir. I have done my B.A. and am engaged in education.

My cousin has been told that Taurus and Aquarius are absolute taboo signs and he cannot give away his testicles to anyone born under those stars as he will suffer for it. Nothing will happen to the oblivious person who is to receive but because the life-giving organ is to be taken into another being and life, we have to do these checks and now I am sorry to inform you that nothing is possible. When you send the certificate of birth that my cousin requires from you, it will be the end and he will close with Wholebody.

This is a very unfortunate ending to our friendship Mr Crookshaky. Sorry,

Your loving friend

Gajan

From **PROJECTFINANCE@hotmail**

Gajan,

I cannot believe your last mail! Why can't you tell your cousin that I am of a suitable star sign and be done with it? I do have a copy of my birth certificate, but I can't see that the date should be of any concern to anyone.

Can't I rely on you to say you have received such a certificate and that it says that I am Libra or whatever.

Please, this is very urgent to me. You have no idea how long my fiancée and I have waited for a suitable donor to be available, as fifty factors seem to be at play in the transfer.

The transplant becomes urgent as our entire plans for the future depend on this procedure and the hopes we have built around it.

Please?

Your friend

Cruikshank

From: **Gajan69@rediffmail.com**

Dear Mr Cruikshank,

At last the right spelling has come. The fellows I got it from wrote anything coming in their heads.

I do want to help you. I think I have a solution. Please send me an authentic copy of your birth certificate.

All sorts of things are available in India which you do not have in the UK. I will get some very professional people here to duplicate the birth certificate with a complete different date while all other particulars remain same. You can even use this at time of entry into hospital in case some other relative of ours start their own investigation. I will then pass off this new certificate to my cousin and his astrological guides and everything will be honky donky. Of course there will be small charge from the forgery people.

I am hoping this puts your mind at rest and give my wishes to your good fiancée.
Your friend
Gajan

From **PROJECTFINANCE@hotmail**
Dear Gajan,
The certificate has been collected by your agent who asked me for £800 to defray the costs of the alterations to the certificate. He told me that part of it would be used for transport to Mumbai and living expenses for you there and some of it was going to the astrologer to keep him from examining and questioning too closely.
I hope this removes all obstacles.
Yours ever
Cru.

From: **Gajan69@rediffmail.com**
Dear Mr Cruikshank,
Congratulations. Your birth date is now officially 15th of March and that makes you a Pisces. Nothing fishy, which is a good joke between friends.
My cousin and his celestial advisor are both pleased and cousin is packing trunks for Delhi where a quick passport agent who has already taken money is alerted for us.
Very soon you will have good news. My fond regards to your wife to be who will rejoice at this chance my cousin is making possible.
Your loyal friend
Gajan

From **PROJECTFINANCE@hotmail**
Dear Gajan,
This is a great relief,
Ever
Edward Cruikshank

From: **Gajan69@rediffmail.com**
Dear Edwrad,
I am writing from Delhi where we are to stay for the time it takes to get passport. A very unfortunate occurrence has happened. My cousin has met with his classmate here who is in political service with the Communist Party (Marxist) and they have gone out drinking one day. My cousin doesn't drink any alcohol. He sometimes takes bhang which is a cooling intoxicating drink made out of milk and Indian hemp on festival days but nothing otherwise.

This wayward communist friend of him made him confess the truth about how he was going to middle east for a transplant donation and the fellow fed him all sorts of political rubbish about the rich world in America and UK buying up the bodies and souls of poor people in India. They came back to our lodgings and I was arguing with them about who would feed children, ideology or hard cash. The miscreant fellow has persuaded my cousin that if he goes to some woman that he knows who is foreign, he can get money from Holland to stop having any operation.

I fear my cousin is now fearing for his ball
to get cut off. The communist chap is always
at our lodgings nowadays.
What to do.
Gajan

From **PROJECTFINANCE@hotmail**
Dear Gajan,
I haven't heard from you for days. What's
going on?
What has the communist chap got to do with it?
Cru.

From: **Gajan69@rediffmail.com**
Dear Edwrad,
We are still in Delhi and rethinking some
things. My friend here, Comrade Sunit is
definitely against the exploitations of third
world for body parts and this kind of
Internet shopping for everything. He is a
very persuasive gentlemen and told us that
the filthy and lonely peoples of the West
are looking for everything on the Internet.
They are buying love like this. They are
doing 'dating agency' selling sex for having
some company, women giving themselves for
being bought dinner and present. Also they
are buying people's body parts. They have
lost all self-respect and exchanging lust
like animals and now have come to capture
our women and men or parts of them.
This is spiritually bad. It means that the
West is bankrupt and broken in spirit and

in body and they have to do colonialism of poor countries. They are buying our girls for marriage and sex from Internet chattings, they are taking kidneys and hearts like cannibals. Comrade Sunit says, and my cousin is believing him like anything, that the East is vital and has what the West is wanting and now the West should start paying for it.

Don't you think he is a very wise man, Comrade Sunit?

Your friend

Gajan

From **PROJECTFINANCE@hotmail**

Dear Gajan,

Of course what Comrade Sunit says is partly true. But you are in education as you told me and you and I, as people without a communist axe to grind, should look at the whole rather than the partial truth. I agree that Comrade Sunit is a wise man and am not surprised that your cousin and you seem inclined to agree with him.

But think of it this way. You and I have made friends through this transaction, haven't we? Can't we put the West and East argument, which is useful politically, behind us and treat one another as friends? I hope that after all this is over we shall be real friends. As I don't even know your cousin's name and have never communicated with him, I don't have any channel of affection towards him, but my dear Gajan, I do seem to want to understand you better and I can predict that you are only half convinced by Comrade Sunit's strong arguments.

I have made myself vulnerable to you as all friends do sometimes. I have told you of Carolyn, my fiancée, and how she has this determined, almost Oriental fixation with having our own child and not through artificial means. It is close to sharing your religious belief in not violating the life spirit, even though she doesn't know it. She feels it.

I have only respect for the feeling that's why I have come so far.

Believe me, Gajan this is my last chance. I am in my late fifties and my last wife, who was ten years younger than myself did abandon me for someone she found – as Comrade Sunit put it – on a dating service provided by the Internet. She took our daughter with her. Comrade Sunit has obviously a great hinterland of knowledge. He is right that in the West I have worked so hard towards gaining material things – I, still a struggling finance advisor – that I neglected my first family and paid the price. Now I am seeking simple happiness with Carolyn and having registered with several agencies for this transplant have been given a chance by Wholebody and your generous cousin for a new life and some future with a family and a child.

Com. Sunit also rounded his argument to you by saying that the West should be made to pay. Perhaps he is right. I have demonstrated my willingness to pay. As I said I want us to negotiate this as friends and therefore want you to come out of it as a happy and willing party. I hope when all this is over you and I will still be in touch and perhaps can even meet. I want then for you and I to look into each other's eyes and recognize humanity there, not exploitation. Please ask your agent to get in touch with me. I have some little token which may help you understand that I am not an exploitative bloodsucker of the West.

And may I ask again? Can you yourself, who matter to me, keep an open mind to my simple argument?

Your friend

Edward

From: **Gajan69@rediffmail.com**

Dear Edrood,

You have written the most persuasive e-mail letter. You are quite right I do see you as a friend. This Comrade Sunit is clever but you may be even cleverer. The Lord Krishna says and it is backed up in our holy Tantric texts, that people can escape their class and caste if they perform certain rituals and good deeds. Yes, I can see Comrade Sunit's point about you being West and we

being East but I am also mightily persuaded
by your argument that certain sacrifices and
actions can make people stand together as
on a plane of eternity, equal and bound to
each other by chains of friendship. And on
that plane, sir, there are no directions,
no East and West and no above and below. Can
you see that?
My agent has conveyed your generosity to me.
Thank you,
Your friend
Gajan

From **PROJECTFINANCE@hotmail**
Dear Gajanji,
I see that we begin to understand each
other. You say you are persuaded by my
arguments. But the crux of the matter is can
you convince your cousin?
I took Carolyn out to dinner last night. It
wasn't a happy occasion. I told her how far
we had got in our communications and I
respectfully related to her all Comrade
Sunit's arguments. Believe me she sympathized
with the main drift of what he is saying,
but she did shed a tear for the way in which
this very argument could disrupt the lives
of two people who only seek in their way a
little happiness.
Your friend
Edward

From: **Gajan69@rediffmail.com**

Dear Edweed,

The fellow Sunit has got a stranglehold. There was big fight between him and me last night in the lodging when he was up to his old tricks and I stood by your argument saying western and eastern could be friends. My cousin was getting persuaded when Sunit the bastard started to resort to fisticuffs. When the fight got bad and I pushed him Sunit fell on one of the partitions in this useless hotel and this same partition crumbled from its attachments and fell on a lady who was sleeping other side. The landlord of the sleeping house heard all the noise when her husband, a Sikh with long hair came to kill us with a knife. The landlord kicked us all out without refund.

It's complete disaster. We have no money. The last you sent me I sent straight to my family and they have no way of returning it. So we are on the street. I am writing this from the Cosmos Internet Café and the only resource which I can immediately think of is some help from you my dear friend. I can get in touch with agent's company in Delhi, staying all night on a park bench or something and calling on them early in the morning if you will do the needful and send just enough money for us to live for a few days and get back with the passport to south. It will also help separate my cousin from Comrade Sunit who is nasty influence. As you

graciously stated early I look upon you as
a friend and who else to turn to in times
like this.
Desperate times
Gajan

From **PROJECTFINANCE@hotmail**
Dear Gajan,
Your agent called with alarming promptness
and I have done the needful as you put it.
Hope it helps.
Edward

From: **Gajan69@rediffmail.com**
Dear Erdwerd,
Cousin and I are in new lodgings thanks to
you. I told him we should buy rail ticket
and go home, but this bastard Sunit has
tacked us down by devious methods even
though I didn't tell him where in the whole
of Delhi we were going. He is now telling
my cousin that the Holland lady will pay him
and to come on their side.
What to do, dear friend?
I am hating Comrade Sunit now.
Your pal
Gajan

From **PROJECTFINANCE@hotmail**
What is the Holland lady willing to pay your
cousin? Surely that's the bottom line.
Cru.

From: **Gajan69@rediffmail.com**
Dear Edrewad,
Despite all my trials my cousin now says he
will go with the Holland lady who is the
communist fellow's main attraction. She has
come to India to talk to all peoples about
taking kidneys and things for western people
just like in our case. She is making a film
about these things and the SUNIT the snake
says she will pay my cousin to be in the
film. They are not saying how much. I know
my cousin too well. He will go with high
bidder, I bet.
Your friend
Gajan

From **PROJECTFINANCE@hotmail**
Gajan,
This is exasperating. What are we to do?
What is your estimate of the payment for his
appearance in the wretched film?
Cru.

From: **Gajan69@rediffmail.com**
Dear Edrawd,
Some light has dawned on the dark horizon.
Forget the payment for the film. Last night
I went and had a drink with the Comrade
Sunit without my cousin. The truth is that
the Sunit is frantically in love with the
Holland lady who is making the film and she
is also encouraging him by having surrendered
herself after he gave her some ganja one

night. He told that she has resisted repeat performances but that she really loves him and is playing very hard for getting. But because SUNIT is in touch with cousin, she needs him. She wants my cousin to appear in the film tomorrow so only one day is left before she returns to Holland but Comrade S says that if we pay for his ticket to Holland and give him some consideration, he will see that my cousin is very disappointed with the Holland lady and the film and all the rot he has heard and will come back in line for the operation. I know you will co-operate with this last step.

No time to waste.

Your dearest friend

Gajan

From: **Gajan69@rediffmail.com**

Dear Ederwad,

The whole plan worked like clockwise. Comrade S was happy with the money and took my cousin aside confidentially to see sights in Delhi. He very cunningly said on their trip that the Holland lady was a real bitch and wanted my cousin to first have the operation and then come for filming as a person who was already a victim of the great organ colonialism. My cousin was surprised as he was thinking prevention is better than complaint afterwards but Sunit told him that this lady thinks on film it would better if he could show his cut off piece or where it used to be after operation. A no-ball location. That way more people would be pitying him.

My cousin got very furious and came back to me. I cunningly said that this was even more evidence of the exploitation when they want to film what they think is horrible and want to pay him for showing his disabilities. So cousin is being persuaded to change his mind again and soon I think, as I have bought tickets out of Delhi, we should go back home and inform Wholebody that passport has been obtained.

Thank you for facilitating this move. The Sunit person was very happy that now his love with the Holland lady has been made possible. I am suspecting that he has a wife he has to leave behind and his conscience is prickling. He said in Holland he will start a Macdonald's franchise or something like that to make big money.

Your friend and facilitator

Gajan Nath

From **PROJECTFINANCE@hotmail**

Dear Gajanan,

Wholebody came through today, in fact within the last half hour and fixed the date of the operation. I want to thank you for all that you've done, even though you never seem to be able to get my name right.

Yours truly

Edward

From **PROJECTFINANCE@hotmail**

Gajanan,

The operation was carried out five days ago as you probably know from your cousin with whom of course I have had no contact though I do know he was in a contiguous operation theatre.

Now may I take up the matter in hand. You probably think that I am a completely gullible fool and that you have taken me for a very long ride to the tune of several thousand pounds. I want to tell you that though I do not doubt the basic veracity of your story, the fact that your family is Tantricly inclined and so on, I do happen to know that a forged birth certificate, even with her Majesty's seal on it should cost in the vicinity of a few hundred rupees, a few pounds, certainly not hundreds or thousands. I want you to know that I didn't for a moment swallow whole your story about communist ideological interference and for all I know you never needed to go to Delhi.

I naturally, as who wouldn't, played along with you and did nothing that would get the co-operation of your family withdrawn allowing you to believe that you were dealing with an eager and naïve Englishman who had fallen into your extortionist trap.

The truth is the opposite. I have lodged all your e-mails with my lawyer and have now sought advice. I shall threaten to sue Wholebody Enterprises for disclosing my case and address to you and recover all the money that you have extorted from me. I realize that having got a little intelligence, you set about to exploit me. Well, you've met your match Mr Gajan which is no doubt not your real name. And I warrant that Wholebody will, when my lawyers get in touch with them, penalize your cousin and family by declining to hand over the whole sum that was agreed between him and them. They will possibly, and I hope they will, deduct what I paid your agent who arrived eagerly on my doorstep each time.

I might add that what you have done amounts to extortion and I can give the police a pretty good description of your agent.

I am writing this knowing that if I had not, I would feel foolish rather than grateful for the rest of my life and of course I am not sure that your agent and you, with your oily assurance of assistance and friendship, would not turn up again with more blackmailing demands. God knows that I don't put it past devious devils such as yourself.

You could of course volunteer to return the money in reply to this mail.

You people may be poor but I feel you have victimized me and my simple wish for a healthy body.

I hope for your sake it doesn't come to criminal prosecution.

Edward Cruikshank

```
From: Mailor-Daemon@rediffmail.com
```
Your mail has been returned unopened. There
was a fatal error in the address.
There is no such account as
Gajan69@rediffmail.com
The original message was received at Sat,
17 May 15:05:01-0400 (EDT)
from root@localhost
—The following addresses had permanent fatal
errors —
Gajan69@rediffmail.com
 —Transcript of session follows—
... while talking to mx2.rediffmail.com.:
<<< 550 Requested action not taken: mailbox
unavailable

JARVIS, JARVIS AND SON, SOLICITORS
13 Theobalds Grove
London WC 1

Dear Edward,

Glad to hear you are recovering and that the surgeon predicts
success.

I have had an extensive correspondence in the last two days
with Wholebody about the matter you put to me.

They profess themselves puzzled. They insist that no breach
of confidentiality took place and that the whole procedure was
routine. Your donor, they insist, was not Indian or of Indian
origin and they have, reserving his confidentiality and entrusting
it to me as a solicitor, made his name, address and particulars
known to me. I can certainly confirm that he was and remains

of European origin and has never travelled to India or anywhere out of Eastern Europe except on the occasion of the operation. As for the party with whom you have been in touch and who has used some leaked knowledge to extract money from you, I can confirm that this is an Indian portal and the man was registered in India with an Indian e-mail address. As you know he has abandoned the address and cleared off. I am told on enquiry that Indian conmen operate this blackmail on very many would-be recipients of donated organs. Our best bet is the police. The fact that he found out that you were to have this operation could have emanated from several sources, including it seems, by your own admission from Carolyn's hairdresser.

Wholebody of course refuse to refund any of the monies paid by you to them for the transfer and consider the matter closed. We must meet and discuss the ramifications of all this when you are feeling better. Meanwhile what shall I do about the police and 'Gajan'?

Yours truly
John Jarvis

During the Long Riots, the Fragrance of Cuticura

Amitava Kumar

THERE ARE LIZARDS IN THE SMALL GARDEN.

I am scared of the girgit. These lizards have long tails although their thin bodies are no longer than the span of my palms. Their colour ranges from pale yellow to dark, scaly brown. Many of them have bloated red sacs under their chin. Although these creatures scare me, I also want to kill them. I often daydream about catching them unawares with a throw, lifting them from their perch with a sharp stone. As they fall back in the air, I imagine seeing their pale, exposed bellies.

Brij Bihari has told me that the lizards are Muslims.

I am suspicious of the lizards with sacs under their chins. These sacs actually used to be beards. During the riots that accompanied the partition of India, the Muslims were running scared from the Hindus. If the Hindus found the Muslims, they would kill them. If the Hindus did not kill the Muslims first, the Muslims would in fact kill the Hindus. Or they would take the Hindus to the new country, Pakistan, where they would be converted and become trapped forever.

Once, the Hindus saw a bearded Muslim running away. They caught him and were about to chop off his head. The man was a coward. In order to save his life, he pointed with his beard toward the well where the other Muslims were hiding. Because of this act of treachery, that man was turned into a lizard with a sac under his chin. That is why when we Hindus look at these lizards they bob their heads as if they are pointing towards a well.

A crack about an inch and a half high separates the bottom of the bathroom door from the cement floor. When Ma takes her bath, I slide my toes under the door and wait. I can hear the water running and the sound of the radio inside.

Whenever Ma notices my feet, she switches off the radio. I hear the clink of her bangles as she comes closer on the other side. I stand with my body pressed against the painted wood, and I can feel on my face my warm breath. A quiet moment passes. And then Ma sprinkles talcum powder on my toes.

No matter how many times this ritual is repeated, I feel surprised and intensely happy. The slight heat of early spring and the smell of talcum powder will evoke in me years later the memory of my childhood.

The giant aerials of All India Radio stand only two hundred yards from our home. Our house is at the end of a short side street. Outside the house, on the left, is a small khataal for cows and buffaloes. The milk that is needed for the neighbourhood comes from this cowshed. Brij Bihari is the owner of the khataal. He is a milkman because that is his caste. His full name is Brij Bihari Yadav. Brij Bihari does not know how to write, but my mother says that he is very smart. He is from Samastipur where he goes by train during the Holi festival.

Ma bathes during that long hour of mid-day after she has finished cooking. She first washes a few clothes and then she fills the buckets for her bath. After Ma emerges from the bathroom – the jingles on the radio announcing her return – we wait for Papa to come home for lunch.

Today, Ma opens the door hurriedly and asks, 'Did Papa call?'

The phone is in the living room. I follow her there. Ma calls my father in his office. I know he is not there because her conversation with Bose Babu, Papa's secretary, goes on longer than is usual. She says, 'You have to arrange for a car. I can't leave Sneha at her school when there is trouble in town.'

My father is an important man. He is the additional magistrate for Patna city. Papa goes to his office in a white Ambassador with the peon sitting in the front seat beside the driver. The peon's name is Raghunath. He holds my father's briefcase in his lap in the car. The driver's name is Aziz. He is an old man. Between Aziz and Raghunath stands propped the Eagle thermos with my father's coffee.

I ask my mother, 'How is it that Didi is allowed to come back early from school?'

My mother says in response, 'Go out and see if Brij Bihari is there. Tell him to come here right now.'

The two buffaloes are sitting at their assigned places outside the khataal. I look inside. It is dark and cool under the thatched roof. I can see the cows, standing in front of their empty tubs, chewing on their cud. But Brij Bihari isn't there. I am about to turn back home when I see Brij Bihari outside the radio station gate talking to two men. I run up and say to him breathlessly, 'Ma is calling you.'

Brij Bihari nods his head but does not move. The men continue to talk in low voices. One of the men has three metal keys and a penknife hanging from the yellow thread that drops in a diagonal across his torso. This man is sitting on the saddle of his bicycle. Brij Bihari and the third man stand on either side of the bicycle. A few minutes pass. At last, Brij Bihari turns and, taking my hand, says, 'Let's go, hero.'

When we get home, Ma is inside standing at the bathroom door listening to the radio. Brij Bihari says to Ma in Hindi, 'There is a storm breaking in the city.'

Ma says, 'They are not telling us much. But they just announced that there is a curfew.'

Brij Bihari says, '*Arre*, the public cannot be controlled by a curfew when it is angry.'

I do not know who the public is. I think of the two men I had just seen talking to Brij Bihari. The one sitting on the cycle perhaps cannot be controlled when he is upset. He uses the small knife hanging from his sacred thread to kill the curfew.

Ma is worried. She has not been able to contact my father. But she doesn't want to use the phone. 'I am afraid he might be calling us here,' she says. Ma is worried about my sister who is four years older than me. Ma tells Brij Bihari why she has called him. 'Take your cycle and go to Sneha Didi's school. Stay there till I am able to send the police. Please do this much for me.'

Brij Bihari laughs at my mother's tone and he tries to set her mind at ease by saying, 'There is nothing to worry about Didi. The public is looking for Muslims.'

But, nevertheless, he is ready to go. My mother says that she will ask for the police jeep to be sent to the school soon. She says, 'Just stay there till it comes.'

I follow Brij Bihari outside. 'The Muslims have been running around a lot. Now the postman is going to come,' he says.

Then, he puts on his cotton vest because he is going to the school. 'A few of the bearded ones,' he says mysteriously, 'are going to be stamped and mailed today.' He points above at the sky. He has a sly look in his eyes, as if he were joking.

Brij Bihari is off quickly on his bicycle.

I can see that the white football that my elder cousin, Pappu Bhaiya, had given me for my last birthday, is still where I had kicked it under the bushes. A single lizard is sitting on it, its tail drooping over the curve of the ball. The lizard makes a swallowing gesture and, for a second, I see its pink mouth. I wonder whether it has eaten an ant.

I like killing ants. There is a matchstick fallen at the edge of the verandah floor near me. I squat down near it and use the matchstick's burnt, black head to slice in half the bodies of the ants that are climbing the yellow wall.

I start with the ant at the bottom and work my way up quickly. But, by then, a new column of ants has started climbing up again, and I have to hurry back to the beginning of the line. This is hard work, but it commands my full attention, and it gives me pleasure. The ants have no idea what I am doing to them. Now and then, however, they break the line and start scurrying in a curve, like the trucks that turn on to a detour when roads are being repaired ahead of them.

I look up and see that the lizard has not moved. I put three dead ants on a small leaf and begin to walk slowly toward the ball on which it sits. But it suddenly disappears on the other side of the football and then I see it diving into the foliage. I place the leaf carefully on top of the ball and slowly retreat to my place next to the wall. I feel like a hunter and I take up the matchstick again.

Once you kill an ant, another ant will eat it. If I keep at this task near the wall, I will have killed enough ants to feed the rest of the ant colony. I have seen ants carrying other ants on their backs. They are not taking the dead ants to be cremated. Brij Bihari has told me that the ants will take the dead ones into their homes and eat them like toast when evening comes.

The ants live in the ground. I would like to see their tiny rooms, one bedroom separated from another, and all linked by thin lines that are actually hallways. In each house, there is a living room where ants sit around and drink tea and eat their dead neighbours whom I have killed.

Brij Bihari is a tall, thin man. His moustache hangs over a part of his face. Brij Bihari's voice comes out from deep inside his stomach, which he holds tight when he walks. He is clad, for most of the time, only in a blue lungi wrapped around his waist. Bare-chested, he roams the neighbourhood with his cows each morning, selling milk door-to-door.

For as long as I can remember, Brij Bihari has been a part of our household. He uses the bathroom in the servant quarters behind our house, and some of his belongings are stored in the garage. In return, my parents use Brij Bihari's services for a variety of tasks. When guests arrive and cold bottles of Coca-Cola need to be brought from the shops near Vijay Chowk, or the doctor needs to be fetched, like the night when my father started vomiting and the phone wasn't working, or when crackers and big chocolate bombs need to be exploded during Diwali, Ma always summons Brij Bihari.

For a few months, we had a maidservant who had come from my mother's village. Her name was Lata. My sister let Lata oil her hair and then weave it into plaits. There was some problem one morning. Lata was upset. My mother had the red toothpowder in her hand – she was still in the middle of brushing her teeth – and she was speaking angrily to Brij

Bihari. Then, my father appeared and asked me to go up to the bedroom. From the window above I later saw Brij Bihari labouring silently in the sun. He was cutting the maize in the back yard.

Lata did not make rotis during lunch that day. When I went to find her, she was lying down on her thin mattress in the small room at the back. The room was next to the bathroom that Brij Bihari and she shared. I asked Lata why she was not in the kitchen and she said, 'I have a stomachache.'

I did not believe her although I did not know why. I said to her, 'I want some water.' She turned her face to the wall and began sobbing. I saw how her back heaved as she wept, and I left the room quickly because I had made her cry. I did not notice that Lata had left our house the next day. It was many days later that I heard Ma telling someone that Lata had returned to her village.

Brij Bihari is very different from my father. Papa is a government officer, and people like Brij Bihari call him saheb. Papa does not joke with anyone. He travels in the car with Aziz and Raghunath, and he finds out from the poor what they want and then he signs files and gives to the people what they need. Aziz, our driver, is a Muslim. I imagine Brij Bihari taking the small and dark-skinned Aziz and putting him in a brown-paper parcel. Stamped and mailed. This makes me think for a moment that I do not have enough air and cannot breathe at all. Now I want Papa to come back home. Didi will be back too. We'll all be unexpectedly together, sitting down for a surprise lunch.

'Tifflin' is the term that Brij Bihari uses for lunch. He cannot really speak English; I laugh when Brij Bihari uses foreign words. One evening, my parents are sitting down in the living room with some guests. Brij Bihari is asked to bring tea. In the kitchen, he holds the tray bearing the teacups in both hands and walks back and forth in the manner of a woman.

Periodically, he stops in front of me. A cup appears in front of me, but before I can take it, Brij Bihari lifts the cup to his pressed lips. He simpers, and says over and over again, 'T.P.' I laugh but feel guilty about laughing at our guests and, perhaps, at my parents.

I am often amused by the way Brij Bihari speaks to me. I do not always understand his meaning. Often, his words are dark and mysterious, like a trapdoor in the floor. From my place in the present, I see myself falling through the door. The dark tunnel opens into the future where, unknown to me, I will struggle to become a writer.

In that distant future, I will find words to describe my childhood. Words will liberate me. But I will also discover a distrust of the promise of language. Words will fail me. I will not be able to undo the confusion around me. One day I will tell myself that I am a writer because the childhood fascination as well as unease with what I am being told has not yet left me. At the place where the trapdoor will finally lead me, people will find words to justify any injustice. People will kill and they will use words to sharpen their knives. Words will join the battle. I will forever be left bereft of language.

In the present, however, in the present of my childhood, which I will later think of as being neither happy nor unhappy, I like talking to Brij Bihari because, unlike my parents, he speaks to me as if I were a part of his world. The world that he lives in is very exciting to me.

My mother knows this and does not like it at all. I have just begun going to school. When I do not write in my notebook, often Ma will say to me, 'What will you do when you grow up? Just milk cows like Brij Bihari?'

I want very badly to take care of Brij Bihari's cows. I want to feed them grass and hay mixed together with a little bit of water in the trough. I like the smell of the hay. I also want to milk the cows, binding their hind legs with rope so that they don't kick at me. I have watched Brij Bihari pulling at their udders so that the milk squirts into the bucket held between his knees. I want to make the milk foam like that. And I want to sleep in the open like Brij Bihari does, on a string cot at night, with the red light atop the aerials above the radio station glowing in the dark like a star.

The police jeep comes to our door and my sister jumps out of it. Brij Bihari is at the back with his bicycle resting on the jeep's footrest. My mother is delighted. She uses her sari to wipe Didi's face. As soon as we are inside the door, Ma kisses Didi. Then, Didi begins to cry and stops only when my mother gives her a glass of water to drink. As abruptly as she had started crying, my sister stops and says, 'I am hungry.'

A constable brings my sister's schoolbag to the door. He is a young man with a steel bangle on his wrist. He seems weighed down by Didi's bag. He says, 'Order hai wapas jaane ka.' The police jeep has been ordered to return. I want it to stay so that I can admire the red lights and the red and blue flag that droops on its hood.

When the jeep is gone, Brij Bihari begins to tell my mother a story. The public is likely to get interested in Sneha Didi's school very soon. The nuns there have begun taking in the Muslim families from the surrounding areas. Brij Bihari has seen this while he waited with his cycle leaning against the giant tamarind tree. Women in burkas with children in tow, all being led by groups of intense young men. The main metal gate at the school is locked. But the side gate is open. The Muslims are using that gate. They are all gathering inside the school's walls.

I know those walls that Brij Bihari is talking about. They are tall and have shards of glass embedded at the top. They are painted white with a red line running around them. The colours are the same as those of my sister's uniform.

My sister says, 'Mother Superior has a very big heart.'

Ma says, 'They have dedicated their lives to the poor.'

Both my mother and sister look a bit like the nuns when they say this. But, Brij Bihari says, 'The Muslims have been building such a big mosque. Why are they not hiding there under their loudspeaker?'

My mother is listening to Brij Bihari as if he has presented her with a puzzle. My sister, however, who knows a lot because she is in school, has a question for Brij Bihari. 'Should the Muslims not have their mosque?'

Brij Bihari is tickled by Didi's question, or maybe by the fact that she knows so little. He begins to speak but my mother has had enough. She says to him, 'What are you saying in front of the children? Have you even fed your cows today? Go to them. . . . At least they do not find differences between Hindus and Muslims.'

This provides Brij Bihari the opening he needs. He says, 'How can you say that, Ma? The cow is our mother. We care for her with our lives, but those Muslims eat cows.'

My mother holds her head in her hands. She says, 'Oh my dear God! Why do you say such things under my roof?'

Brij Bihari laughs. He says, 'Ma! This is the plain truth. We wouldn't have these riots if the Muslims had any sense. How can you like them if they kill cows?'

When Brij Bihari leaves, there is a discussion about whether we should wait longer for Papa. My mother feeds me while Didi eats by herself. Ma has cooked fish. She removes the bones and I mix the fish with the rice. When I eat my food, I think of the Muslims who instead of goats or chicken eat cows.

The phone rings. But, it is not my father. It is someone from his office who wants to know if Papa has come home. My mother says she has no news. Ma asks the caller what 'the situation' is like in the town. She listens to the answer and sighs. Then, she returns to the business of feeding me.

It is hours before my father comes home. My mother has not eaten. Raghunath comes in first with the briefcase and the Eagle thermos. Didi takes the flask from him but I run out to find my father. Papa is talking to Brij Bihari, who is telling him about Didi's school. My father takes my hand and leads me into the house.

My mother is angry. She will not speak to my father. She puts a plate in front of him when he sits at the table. Papa asks my sister, 'The jeep came for you at school, little one?' My sister nods but doesn't say anything because she knows Ma is angry.

Ma puts fish in the bowl for Papa. He begins eating. Ma says, 'Was there not a single phone anywhere for you to tell us where you were and when you would come home?' My father looks at me and my sister. He does not look at my mother or bother to reply. His face becomes stern and he begins to eat more quickly.

Ma goes to the door and asks Raghunath very loudly, 'Do you want some tea? And where is Aziz?'

Now my father breaks his silence. He says, 'You want to offer tea to a man whose house is burning?' His tone is not very kind. He is still not looking at my mother. He says, 'It was dangerous even to keep Aziz in the car. I went and dropped him in his neighbourhood. There have been police firings. At least twenty-two men have been killed.'

My mother stays silent. I do not understand what I am hearing my father say. I do not like how my parents are behaving. In order to break the silence, I ask my father, 'Papa, why does Aziz kill cows?'

A dark shadow passes over my father's face. I can see that I have made him angry. He turns in great fury toward my mother and demands loudly, 'What have you been telling the boy?' This confuses me. I can see it also confuses my mother. There is such immense sadness on her face as she looks for a moment at my father.

My mother holds the edge of the green curtain close to her. She has turned her face slightly as if she has been slapped. I walk close to Ma and put my arms around her waist. My forehead touches her cool stomach. My mother is sobbing. I press my nose against my mother's sari and wait for her to gently place her hand on my head.

The jeep has returned to take my father back for patrolling. At the back of the jeep are the police constables wearing khaki shorts and red berets. They sit like roosters crammed in a bamboo basket. The men are silent. They have dark, sweaty faces and they look at me without much curiosity.

The driver, also in khaki, has a revolver in his belt. The driver is the only one standing outside the jeep. My father is having lemon tea in the verandah of the house, and the driver is calmly watching us. I call the driver into the garden; my father turns his head, as if to ask why, but then turns away again. He is listening to the radio.

I ask the driver if I can hold his revolver. The man pats it and points wordlessly at my father. He shakes his head as if to say that Papa will be angry.

I say to him, 'Are you a Hindu or a Muslim?'

The driver reaches into his shirt and takes out a ragged sacred thread. He asks me, 'Why do you call me a Muslim?'

'And they?' I point toward the soldiers in the jeep.

'Woh hamaare hee ladke hain,' he says. They are all our boys.

I understand that the police are there to protect my father. My father is invincible. I look at him as he sits on a cane chair without his shirt, listening to the news on the radio and sipping tea. I ask the driver if my father also has a gun. The man says, 'Why does he need a gun if we are there with him?' He uses the English word 'command' to tell me that the men will use their guns when Papa orders them to.

I know now that no one can harm my father because he is an officer. But in case anyone dares to try, I have decided that this is how the plan will work: if the attackers are Hindu, the policemen will simply tell them that Papa is also a Hindu; and if a Muslim rioter threatens my father, the policemen in the jeep will shoot him down.

My sister is doing her homework. Ma has asked me to sit down with my own picture book on the sofa. Didi is wearing in her hair the elastic band with shiny plastic stones that Rani Aunty has given her. Such bands are called 'Love-in-Tokyo.' I have in the past asked my sister about the name but she has just shrugged her shoulders.

When I go down to the kitchen, I see that Brij Bihari is standing near the doorway talking to my mother. He is telling her that a few Muslim families have collected inside the walls of the radio station nearby.

I ask him, 'Will they attack us?'

Brij Bihari says, 'They have their tails between their legs.'

Maybe the Hindus will set fire to the whole radio station, I think.

Brij Bihari tells my mother that it is because there is a police party in the radio station that the Muslims have come there.

Ma says, 'I am thinking of Aziz. . .I hope his family is safe.'

And then it is morning. I find myself coming down the stairs. The sun is out. I remember the previous night and the troubles of the day only when I see Brij Bihari once again standing outside the kitchen. Nothing appears to have changed. Ma is inside making tea. Brij Bihari is holding one of his milk cans, which he bounces lightly against the back of his leg. I ask him, 'Did they burn the radio station?'

'No, no,' Brij Bihari laughs as he says this, and takes me by the hand out into the garden to show me the yellow building, which is standing there with its tall aerials, unharmed.

My father, I discover, has already left with the police party. I want to know when Papa is going to come back, and Ma says, 'He'll come for lunch. Things are returning to normal.' I look at my sister. She has planted a small peepul plant in a pot. It has a single leaf that is fresh green in colour. My sister is using a small comb to dig the soil in the pot. She then takes water from the sink in her hand and pours it on the dirt around the plant.

When my father comes for lunch, there are no discussions about the riots. When Didi asks him when her school is going to open, my father says, 'Monday.'

I ask them what day it is today, and my sister says, 'He doesn't know anything at all.' When Papa looks up at her from his plate, Didi says, 'Friday.'

Next week Didi will go back to school then. My mother has told me I will begin going to school in July. I will be five years old. I will be in K.G. for two years. Didi says that my teacher will be Mrs Joseph.

I ask Papa, 'When I start going to school, will a police jeep take me there?'

My father smiles at me. His smile shows that he loves both my sister and me. He says, 'Do you want to go with the police? Can't Aziz take you in our car?'

Is Aziz still alive?

I ask my father, 'Is Aziz going to come back?'

My father says, 'He has to drive our car. Where will he go?'

My sister speaks up now. She asks, 'Didn't you say to Ma yesterday that his house was burning?'

Papa says, 'No. . . . That's not what I said. It is Friday today. He gets the afternoon off for prayers.'

My sister says, 'Did you see him today?'

Papa says, 'My dear, today people are still settling down after the troubles in the town last night. I know Aziz is fine. I know the area he lives in. . . . Eat your food.'

One morning, indeed, Aziz is there, passing a cloth over the white Ambassador car. Raghunath and Brij Bihari stand chatting with each other near the khataal. I go out to the gate of the house. A few feet to my left, almost within my reach, there is a lizard sitting on the hedge. I do not go any further and call out to Aziz. I say, 'Aziz, why did you not come all these days?'

Aziz says, 'Beta, bahut aafat thi shehar mein.' Son, there was a lot of trouble in the town.

I watch Aziz working on the car. Then, Ma calls out for the thermos to be taken out and Raghunath hurries inside. When my father steps out with a few files in his hand, Aziz opens the car door for him and asks Raghunath to get in. The car leaves. It is then that Brij Bihari, leaning over the gate with a twig in his hand, tells me that Aziz has spent these last few days at his sister's house. The sister is an attendant in Kurji Holy Family Hospital. Her husband had been killed in a riot five or six years ago, and she lives with her daughter near the Patthar Wali Masjid.

I ask Brij Bihari, 'Will Aziz now return to his own house?'

He says, 'How can he? The public threw kerosene on it and burnt it to the ground.'

Brij Bihari looks serious. But he must be joking! When I look at him, I know that what he is saying is true. He looks sad too. What will my parents say when they hear this?

'What happened to his clothes? Did they get burnt also?'

Brij Bihari says, 'Ek photo tak nahin bacha paya.' He could not even save one photograph.

I want to go inside the house now. It seems to me that it is hot outside. I tell Brij Bihari that I will talk to my parents about Aziz. Brij Bihari laughs. He says, 'What will you tell them that they don't know? Ma has given him two of saheb's shirts.'

'Really?'

I cannot feel angry with my parents for not telling me about Aziz. My father was not able to save the house of the man who works for him. I feel confused by this, and am suddenly filled with disappointment. I am sad for Aziz but I also realize that my father is not who I think he is. He is helpless, just like me. It is even possible that he is scared of the lizards that sit on our fence. I am a little bit ashamed, and I want to cry.

Brij Bihari looks at his khataal. He says, 'Aziz has to travel a good distance to come here every morning. I am trying to sell him my bicycle. I will be like the bank. He will pay me a monthly rate.' He laughs. And adds, 'Aziz is a driver. I think he will keep the cycle in a good condition.'

More than thirty years have now passed. I went to the house about six months ago. It stands unchanged but everything else around the house has altered beyond recognition. The yellow walls of the radio station are now no longer visible behind the tall buildings that have come up all around it. In place of the khataal now stands a brown concrete structure from where you can buy milk by putting tokens in a machine. A part of the field where I later played cricket has been turned into a shopping complex with stores selling suitcases, television, and ice cream. There is a huge sign outside with an Omega watch, the hands fixed at two o'clock. The other half of the field is taken by a new Hanuman Temple. It is surrounded by fluorescent lights that are attached to banana leaves. The leaves are made of concrete and have been painted green. They sprout out of black pillars. On the dome of the temple sits a large grey megaphone.

One day during my visit, I was in a pharmacy buying some Benadryl. A man standing next to me asked the shopkeeper for a tin of Cuticura talcum powder. I was suddenly reminded of my childhood. I was a little boy again. I saw the warm corners of my mother's smile and caught the scent of her smell as she passed from one room to another in that first house in Patna. In that stuffy shop, already getting filled with the darkness of the evening, I even imagined I could hear the radio.

In March this year, when I read of the riots, I remembered that evening in the shop in Patna. I thought of my parents. But, I have been away too long because along with those memories – of the violence that I barely understood, or of the ways in which we related to each other – came the thought that the name Cuticura sounds so oddly Indian, fitting in nicely with words like *raita* or *tanpura*.

Naina

Shauna Singh Baldwin

NAINA HAS CARRIED HER BABY INSIDE HER SO LONG, SHE cannot remember the day her fullness began. She remembers Dr Johnson – just out of medical school, then, apple-cheeked, without her streak of grey – Naina remembers her, cold disc of the stethoscope pressed to Naina's mounding stomach, listening, shaking a very solemn head. 'Any day now.'

And Naina remembers the due date, her heels wide apart in stirrups, remembers every moment of excruciating pain from pushing, pushing, and nothing coming out, not even blood. That she remembers. Then the unwilled dilation, more pushing, more pushing. The brown balloon of her stomach trembling as her baby retreated from light.

She remembers refusing the knife that would have sliced from navel to her mound of spiky black hair. Refusing so loudly, signing papers, more papers, and no one from the Family near her. She remembers her own voice, fourteen years younger, still imitating Asha Bhonsle's soprano because that's all Daddyji ever played on the tape recorder, screaming, 'Leave her. When she's ready, she'll come'. . .the pitying whispers of nurses; all the young doctors, crowding about her bed to discuss her case.

'I am not a case,' she screamed. 'Please, please go away.'

Naina knew it was a girl from the very beginning. Dr Johnson didn't have to show her the pictures – pieces of sky collaged to black plastic. Only a girl would be so comfortable in her mother's womb that coming out and needing to grow would spoil her world. By then Naina had talked to the baby so many months – now so many years – that if the baby hadn't been a girl before she took residence in Naina's womb, she surely became one.

Dr Johnson confirmed it every month, and by now she uses the same words she used last month, last year. 'Yes, I can hear her; her heartbeat is regular. Here,' pinning an x-ray to the light box on the wall, 'see where her toes curl and look at her hands! Still so tiny after fourteen years.'

Also every month, for the past two years, Dr Johnson says, 'That Chinese woman called again to ask if you want her help.' It's the one who says she was a sinseh doctor, and who is repeating her whole medical degree and training so that she can practise in Canada. 'She swears she's not connected to *Guinness* or *The Globe* or *Star* or the *National Enquirer*. . .whenever she calls, I tell her we'll think about it.'

By now all the tabloids have written their pieces, had their say. The journals of medical research have taken note, moved on to the next freak show. They still follow up, once in a while, despite Naina's unlisted phone number.

Naina turns wide eyes upon Dr Johnson, and the bindi above them is a third eye that has become wary of the word 'help'. 'My baby will come when she is ready,' she says, as she has every year.

Dr Johnson paces, 'What is it in your genetic makeup – what is preserving this baby?' Her tone says Naina is being stubborn, refusing to provide critical information. 'All the specialists I've referred you to, all the psychotherapists. . .I can't think what to do next.'

Naina opens her mouth; Dr Johnson breaks in, 'I won't override your wishes, Naina. Unless I think the child is at risk – amazing that all the tests show no danger there. Just amazing. Well,' with a sigh, 'if it's not hurting you or hurting the baby, I suppose there's no harm. Two can live as cheaply as one. But upon my word, it's a strange phenomenon!'

Naina pulls her heels from the stirrups and rises from vinyl padding. Dr Johnson leaves her alone to dress.

In the reception, Naina folds the leg of her salwar about her calf and jams her stockinged feet into moon-boots. She struggles into her coat, draws the scratchy wool of her scarf across her neck as if she were adjusting a dupatta across her shoulders. Dupattas are passé in India now, her cousin-sister Sunita says, but Daddyji insisted she wear one growing up in Malton; the scarf has become a substitute dupatta.

It's no different every time. The weight of her belly pressing against maternity underwear, the baby's pull on the placenta coiled within her. She stands at the bus stop for a while, till her nose freezes; then she trudges to the subway, emerges three blocks from the boulangerie.

André, the landlord, is coming down the staircase, a tray of petits pains levitating over his head as he descends to meet her, 'Want one?'

'No. Merci, André.' His apron leaves flour-streaks on her coat as he brushes past.

The day Stanford moved out, André didn't offer her petits pains. 'You could lose a little weight, a young woman like you. Get a haircut, buy some sexy clothes at the Eaton Centre. One date with a jeune homme, you'll forget all about Monsieur Stanford. I'll talk to Celeste, she'll know a few good guys.' He meant to be comforting. When reporters besieged the boulangerie, André kept his opinion to himself ('they're good customers') and he met them stone-faced, arms folded across his chest, on this very staircase – 'No trespassing, mes amis.'

Busy in her loft studio, Celeste, André's wife, never found Naina a few good guys, but counselled in brief appearances on the landing, holding hands mottled with clay high above her denim smock, 'Ça ne fait rien, Naina, mon ami! Some things, they take years. This one I work on now – a lifetime. A lifetime, it take me. I try and I try, mais. . .' Celeste's sculpture is realist, the figures so lifelike that when a caretaker statue she sculpted was exhibited at the Royal Ontario Museum, people stopped to ask it directions.

Mothering, Baby Care, Working Mother magazines besiege Naina's door. She doesn't remember subscribing; money is not for spending on subscriptions, money is for saving. But the magazines still arrive, as if they know she hasn't delivered yet.

Delivered.

She has delivered so many other things in her thirty-five years, why can she not deliver the girl? Delivering is giving, from the sender to the receiver. The woman who delivers just the conduit along the way. One job she had, soon after Stanford left, was delivering parcels. She discarded her bright kameez and salwar for the drab brown slacks and shirt of a UPS uniform. Perched high above cars in her cab, long hair wound into a tight bun and hidden away under the cap. Till the dispatcher said he couldn't understand her accent on her call-ins and she might as well forget it because it wasn't his fault she heard 'Ramana' when he'd said 'Ramada'.

Naina turns the key, flicks the light switch. Not much here, but something to call her own. A lumpy Murphy bed, its two legs permanently lowered to the parquet floor, a desk and chair she and Stanford bought together at a junk dealer on Spadina, books piled on a low-legged piri from the Family home in Malton. A yeasty smell rises around her from the boulangerie below.

She lowers her weight to the seat in the bay window that bulges over Edgewood Street, not bothering to raise the blinds.

The ache again, at the small of her back.

When I know who sent you, baby, then I'll know to whom I must deliver you. But till then, you stay with me, achcha?

Sunita – 'call me Sue' – is svelte in a sage green polo-neck tunic and black tights. Coming as emissary from her aunt, Naina's mother, like a finger extended outdoors to test a chill wind, she is the only one who still comes to see Naina from the Family. She has nothing to gain, Naina reminds herself, nothing at all by driving all the way east and spending several toonies to park her white BMW in the parking lot across the street.

Nothing to gain, but satisfaction.

'Why don't you tell your Daddyji "sorry" – buss! That's all it takes. One little word and you can be back ek dum, immediately. No problem. . .'

But this is the problem.

'I have done nothing wrong,' says Naina. 'All I committed was love. There is too little of it, so I felt it. Enough for all of us.'

'Love, shove,' Sunita's laugh could peel paint from the dingy blue walls. 'What happened to your gora guy, now? Not that I'm saying you did anything wrong, mind you – you were just young and foolish. All I'm saying is now you should say sorry. Then we can all meet together – none of this, "I can't tell anyone I'm going to see Naina, but everyone knows and gives me secret messages for her." So I'm just asking, does it hurt you to say it, or what?'

'No,' says Naina. 'Saying sorry would not hurt my flesh. It would not break a bone. It will not make me bleed. It will not kill me, that is true. But, Sunita, I am *not* sorry. It's important to me to mean what I say.'

'Call me Sue,' Sunita says automatically. Then continues, 'But I ask you, what is the harm in *saying* it? What does it cost you? Just to please everyone.' A frustrated click of the tongue. 'You really have no sense, Naina. Fourteen years! Even Ram returned home after fourteen years' exile.'

'He was a god, he was a king – men can return home once they do what they have to do.'

'Such funny ways you see things, Naina. All this women's libber talk, see where it brought you?' Sue's hand rising to her nose ring, jingles a wristful of twenty-two carat gold bangles. 'Lose a little weight,' she advises kindly, three-inch heels clopping to the apartment door. 'Otherwise, even if you make up, how will Uncle and Aunty find you a match? They'll have to find a widower or even a divorced fellow now, but still you have a chance. Then you can have children just like mine. Think what I'm saying – one little word.'

The baby shifts appreciatively as Sunita leaves. A tiny fist punches suddenly, stretching Naina's lost abdomen. She strokes it, crooning, 'Chanda mama dur ke. . .'

In the evening, Naina takes the baby in her stomach, her hat, mittens and a coat, and climbs on the 509 streetcar. Downtown, she rises in a carpeted cell to the top of a tinted glass skyscraper. There she bends and straightens, emptying garbage cans and sorting paper from plastic to ready it for rebirth. She wipes a rag gently around computers brooding in suspended mode in the corner of each empty cubicle. The roar of her vacuum fills empty hallways, sucking up dirt. She straps on golden-yellow kneepads to kneel and polish the expanse of wood floors in corporate meeting rooms.

The white fluorescence hums, 'Good money, good money.'

That's what André said when he gave her the card. 'It's good money.' Said it kindly, having printed off three late fee notices in a row, to slip beneath her door. Naina looked at the card, heart falling, realizing she was being given an option the Family would find even less to their liking; the Family is not of that caste of people who clean for others.

But André was being kind, and he did not know the Family or its deep disgust for people who clean. And so Naina looked past the Family and called the number on the card.

'It's just temporary,' she told the baby. 'Till you are ready to come into the world.'

Emptying trash, she wonders at what point in the past four or five years had the cleaning become permanent? Become an important job that deserves a dedicated army, instead of a cleaning crew or two. She can aspire higher with her college degree – anyone in the Family would. But she's used to this now, it gives her mind space as her hands move, and no one demands she wear a dress or pants, or hide her long black hair under a khaki cap.

It's important work that must be done each night, to offset the white-collar crimes of the day.

Stanford wore a white collar, even in those days when they were just students. And a suit. To class. They met at a Mmuffin stand and her love reached out by itself, extended beyond the

Family to enfold him, when he admitted to feeling as foreign in Toronto as she did. It took months for her to understand he felt foreign because of 'all these people from other countries coming to Canada, taking over all we've built'. It was Stanford who rented the apartment above the boulangerie, winking at André as he rolled out his bearskin rug, set his poufy chair before his stereo. Rented it because he said it made him feel like a thief every time he had to park a block away from her home so Daddyji wouldn't find out she was dating a gora.

Daddyji found out, of course. Found out when her belly began growing. Her mother told Daddyji, 'This is Canada, these things happen.'

'But not to my daughter,' raged Daddyji. 'Have you taught her no better?'

Then Naina saw her mother's face close, close to Naina like the door her father slammed in her face.

After graduation, Stanford took his stereo, his poufy chair and his bearskin rug, and moved to Seattle, gambling on a free-trade future without encumbrances. 'Mistakes happen,' he said. 'You take responsibility, you move on. I'll send you money when the child comes.'

He never did, for the child has never been delivered.

He probably thinks Naina got rid of it. Stanford, proud wearer of the yuppie label every day of the eighties, reads the *Wall Street Journal,* not the *National Enquirer*, or the *Journal of Medical Research*.

Who sent you, baby? Where shall I deliver you?

Naina spends her mornings with her swollen feet up on the radiator, watching snow come down on Edgewood Street, imagining tropical breezes. 'You're so smart, baby. No reason to come out into this weather.' She pats her stomach as a ring quakes the cordless phone.

'That woman I told you about?' Dr Johnson sounds surprised. 'She called again. She still thinks she can help you. She's so insistent, Naina, I think you should see her. I'll tell her she must come here. It can't do any harm. It may address the psychological effect this is having on you.'

'I'm fine, I don't need to see anyone.'

'Naina, listen to me! We've tried everything else for your case.'

'I'm not a case.'

'Well, you will be a case if this continues. How's next Friday?'

'Bad.'

'Naina, I'm trying to help. We don't know what effect your decision to allow nature to take its course may have on the baby. There could be brain damage after this long, there could be personality problems.'

'I still say – why are you not listening? – I still say: when my baby is ready, she will come.'

'All right, let's look at it your way – don't you want to know, Naina? Don't you want to know what she's waiting for? Why she's waiting so long? This Doctor – Mrs – Chi says she can help us understand that.'

Naina said, 'Maybe.'

'Next Friday, then. Be here at ten.'

Baby, talk to me. Only to me. Tell me where you come from. Say where I must deliver you.

'My hypnosis is not covered by Ontario Health, you have to pay in advance – oh, doesn't matter; we can worry about that later.' The young doctor, a well-kept petite woman of about forty-five, is Cantonese Chinese. Jovial, not earnest – Stanford used to say all Chinese people are earnest.

But then Stanford didn't know very many Chinese people. Stanford didn't know Dr Chi.

Dr Chi is the first doctor Naina has ever talked to who has not made her repeat her entire medical history for her questions. It could be she read it before she met Naina, the simplest explanation, but the least likely. It feels as if Dr Chi just *knows;* she has not asked Naina a single stupid question. For instance, whether her decision not to allow a knife near her belly is occasioned by vanity or whether it is – delicate pause – her Hindu religion? Dr Chi has asked her to lie down, not on the vinyl-padded table with her heels in the stirrups, but on a couch in Dr Johnson's consulting room.

'I think you must ask the baby why she refuses to be delivered.' Dr Chi flicks a stray lock of straight black hair from her eyes; Naina catches a whiff of Tiger Balm.

'She does not come because she is not ready,' repeating her standard explanation.

'And we could ask her if she were delivered by Cesarean operation, would she die?'

'Why should she answer you?' Naina asks, a little jealous.

'No reason, no reason – quite right. No, she will speak through you.' Dr Chi pauses, rubs her hands though the room is warm and the snow is outside, falling fast.

'You will use me to ask my baby to speak?'

'Yes, yes, of course. How else can it be done?' she pats Naina's arm, gives a Buddha-smile. 'Lie still, now, lie still. Allow yourself to relax,' says Dr Chi.

Allow myself?

The couch is soft beneath Naina's shoulders. The baby's weight settles above her. A cobweb hangs above where walls and white ceiling meet. Naina holds her belly, rubs it soothingly, closes her eyes. Dr Chi's Tiger Balm scent grows stronger.

'You are back where you were born, far from Canada. There's no snow outside. . .it's warm, even hot. Getting hotter. The heat is so strong it sears your eyeballs, you remember that kind of heat? Yes. . . . Allow yourself to feel your eyes become heavy. . .getting heavier. Smell the fragrance of dust, feel a nice breeze cooling your skin. . .?'

'Yes.'

'Allow your limbs to feel heavier and heavier. . .you're going deeper into yourself.' Dr Chi's voice flattens, 'You are looking within your womb. There, in the dark. . .you see her yet? Yes? See if you can move towards her. Ah, you are there? Ask her the questions you have in your heart. . .'

Naina can see her, very small, comma-shaped, brown-skinned, black-haired. She opens her arms. . .

Do you know me, baby? I am your mother.

I know you. I have known you a long time.

Why do you wait within me? Wait so long? Make me carry you everywhere?

I wait because you are not ready to receive me.

I thought it is because you were not ready to come to me.

You were wrong.

I am ready, baby. What can I promise you that will bring you to birth?

Tell me you will love me into being. Tell me you will not be afraid.

That would be untrue, baby.

Then tell me you will live with your fear and your doubt and even so, bring me to light.

Why have you chosen me for your birthing?
Kismat, the luck of the draw.
Who sends you to me?
The unknown.
Will you come by the knife or will you come without?
I will come when you are open wide and deep as a well.
To whom shall I deliver you, baby?
To life, to the world.
What if I fail you, baby?
You do not fail me if you try your best.
I will try.

Dr Chi's Buddha-smile is above her. 'Oh, your bindi is smudged,' she says kindly. 'It was weeping.'

The prescription Dr Chi writes for Naina is for a broth of chicken, laced with ginger juice and brandy, to be washed down nightly with red date tea.

Naina's baby is born in October on Diwali day, the day Ram came home from exile. Few diyas burn on the windowsills of homes, and there are no sparklers; few celebrate this festival in Toronto. The child comes quietly, from an unwitnessed, private labour. Labour that was joy, joy that was labour. There is no one but Naina to staunch the blood, clean the child, cut the cord and offer the gods her thanks.

All my thanks, heartfelt thanks.

And in the morning, Naina opens her door to Celeste who cries, 'Cherie, I finished it, come and see . . .! *Oh, la la!* What have we here?'

The bay window encircles Naina as she resumes her seat, the baby at her breast.

'Ah, your bébé and mine, they came together! I have work all night as if a beam had opened between myself and le bon dieu.'

'I, too, worked all night,' says Naina, smiling radiantly. 'I'll come up and visit yours soon.'

When Celeste is gone, Naina lifts the cordless phone.

It's time she told the Family; she'll call Sunita – really shock her this time. Time she found Stanford and surprised him, tell him what she's done without his help. Time to register the hybrid little being in her arms.

The Tailor

Rana Dasgupta

NOT SO LONG AGO, IN ONE OF THOSE SMALL, CAREFREE lands that used to be so common but which now, alas, are hardly to be found, there was a prince whose name was Ibrahim.

One summer, the usual round of private parties and prostitutes became too tedious for Ibrahim and he decided to go on a voyage around the provinces of the kingdom, 'to see how those villagers spend all their damned time'. So he packed clothes and American one-dollar bills (for letting fly from the windows of his jeep) and set off with his young courtier friends in a jostling pack of father-paid cars, whooping and racing.

Despite themselves, the young men fell silent when the ramshackle streets of the outskirts of the city finally gave way to open countryside. The smooth, proud highways built under the reign of Ibrahim's grandfather began to loop up into the hills and, as the morning mists cleared, the city boys looked out on spectacular scenes of mountains and forests. For several hours they drove.

By early afternoon they had travelled a great distance without a single halt, and as they approached a small town Ibrahim pulled off the road and stopped. The scene was all polo shirts and designer jeans amid the slamming of car doors, the stretching of limbs, the pissing behind bushes – and the townsfolk quickly gathered to find out who these visitors were. 'Certainly they are film stars come to make videos like on MTV,' they said to each other as the band of young men strode into the main square of the town, sun glaring from oversized belt buckles and Italian sunglasses. Goats and chickens whined and clucked their retreats, as if to clear the set.

On the minds of the young men was food; and very soon orders had been placed, chairs brought from front rooms and the local inn, and they were sitting sipping coconut juice in the shade of a wall. Around the square, the whole town stood and watched. Children stared, shop owners came out onto the streets to see what was going on – and a number of youths who were no younger or older than these visitors stood wondering who the heroes could be, and committing to memory every gesture, accoutrement, and comb-stroke.

The food was brought and Ibrahim and his companions began to eat vigorously. The boldest of the villagers stepped forward and addressed them,

'Please, kind Sirs, tell us: Who are you?'

None of the courtiers knew what to say. Which was more sophisticated: to tell the truth, or to remain silent?

Ibrahim himself spoke.

'We have come from far away, and we are very grateful for your kindnesses.'

What a fine answer that was! The local people felt their civic pride swell, and the prince's companions thought once again to themselves, 'That is why I am me and he is a prince.' As women brought more and more food, the sun's rays seemed to glow more yellow with the harmony that could exist between these two groups who seemed to have so little in common.

The meal was over; and with much wiping of hands and mouths the party left their plates and large piles of dollars behind and began to explore the narrow streets of the town, followed by a crowd of excited townsfolk.

They saw small houses with children playing and women sweeping, stalls piled high with fruit and vegetables, and shops of shoemakers, butchers, and carpenters. Finally, at the end of an alleyway, they came to a little store hung out front with robes and dresses: the tailor.

'Let's see what this fellow has to offer,' said Ibrahim. A bell rang as they opened the door, and they pushed past it into a gloomy room overflowing with clothes. The tailor rushed forward to greet them.

'Come in, come in gentlemen, plenty of room, please!' He hastily pushed things out of the way to make space for them to stand. 'What can I do for you?'

'What is your name, tailor?' asked Ibrahim.

'Mustafa, at your service, Sir.'

'You live here alone?'

'Yes.'

'And what do you make?'

'I make anything and everything that can be worn. The people here are poor, so mostly it is simple work. Cotton dresses for the ladies. Shirts for the men. But I can see you are grand visitors. I will show you something special.'

He went to the back of his store and took out a large packet wrapped in brown paper. The young men drew around as he reverentially laid it out on the workbench and untied the string. He slowly unwrapped it, and there, inside, glowing with pent-up light, was the most magnificent silk robe any of them had ever seen. Cut in the traditional style, it was intricately patterned, delicately pleated, and slashed on the sleeves and flared skirts to reveal exquisite gold brocade beneath. The web of stitches that covered the whole robe, holding it in its perfect shape, was entirely invisible, and all the sections fitted together without a single break in the pattern.

The men stared, taken aback at this unexpected splendour.

'This is a fine piece of work, tailor. There are too few people in our country who have respect for these old traditions,' said Ibrahim.

'Thank you, Sir. This is the achievement of my lifetime. It has taken me years to save the money to make this. It was my own little dream.'

Ibrahim gently felt the textures of the shimmering robe.

'Tailor, I would like you to make me a robe even more magnificent than this.'

Ibrahim's companions were amazed. Was he in earnest? They had never seen this seriousness in him.

More amazed still was the tailor himself.

'I am deeply honoured, Sir, at your request. But may I ask first – please do not misunderstand me – who you are and whether you are sure you can afford what you ask for. These materials come from far away and are now very rare. I will need to travel to meet with merchants. They will have to send out orders far and wide. It will take six months, and – '

'Do not worry. I am Ibrahim, eldest son of King Saïd. I will see that your expenses are covered and you yourself are handsomely paid for your pains. Please embroider the robe with the royal stag and crescent moon, and deliver it to the royal palace when it is finished.'

The tailor was moved.

'Your Highness, I will do what you ask. You will not be disappointed. I will make the most splendid robe you have ever seen, and I will bring it myself to your palace.'

'I thank you, tailor. I have every confidence in you.'
And with that, they left.

For several weeks the tailor did not sleep as he made the arrangements for the new robe. First of all he needed a bank loan to cover the enormous costs of the materials he was to buy. Luckily, news of the fabulous order had immediately spread across the town and the quiet tailor had acquired a new fame. Within a few days he had managed to find funds and take on an assistant to help with the work. He set off immediately on a tour of the surrounding towns to look at the finest fabrics, and when nothing was satisfactory he sent the incredulous merchants away to find better. Normally a thrifty and reclusive man, the tailor suddenly became bold and extravagant in the accomplishment of this fantastic project. He bought books of old artworks to ensure he had understood every nuance of the traditional styles. The usually silent alleyway outside his shop became crowded with the vans and cars of merchants bringing samples and deliveries. The racks inside were packed away to make space for the accumulating piles of luxurious silks and brocades.

He meditated on the antique familiarity of the royal crest until it came to life in his head as a magnificent design: while the stars circled at the edges and a grand city twinkled in the distance, the whole chain of animal life arranged itself among the trees to gaze upon the stag who stood alone in a clearing, silvery in the silken light of the crescent moon.

For days at a time the tailor would not move from his workbench as he drew and cut, pinned and sewed. New lamps were brought in to allow him to carry out the intricate work at night, and with astonishing rapidity the flimsy panels of silk assembled themselves into a robe as had not been seen since the days of the old court. After four months the job was finished, and the robe was carefully laid out in the workshop, complete with its own shirt, pantaloons, and matching slippers. The tailor rented a small van, loaded up his precious cargo, and set out for the capital city.

The skies were full of the radiant expectation of morning when the tailor made his approach to the royal palace. In the busy streets trestle tables were juddered and clacked into readiness, and a procession of vans spilled forth the goods that would festoon their surfaces: sparkling brassware, colourful fabrics, beeping alarm clocks, and novelties for tourists. People were everywhere. Men smoked and talked by the side of the road, waiting to see how the day would progress, village women found patches of ground to arrange displays of woven bedspreads and wicker baskets, and boys hawked newspapers full of morning conversation.

As he drove through the unfamiliar streets the tailor felt elated by the crowds. 'What wonders can be achieved here!' he thought to himself. 'Everywhere there are great buildings housing unheard-of forms of human pursuit, new things being made and bought and sold, and people from all over the world, each with their own chosen destination. Even the poor know they are treading on a grander stage: they look far into the future and walk with purpose. What clothes might I have made had I spent my life here!'

The road leading to the royal residence was generous and pristine, with lines of trees and fountains converging in the distance on the domed palace that already quivered in the heat of the morning. The tailor stared at the big cars with diplomatic license plates, marvelled at the number of people that worked just to keep this street beautiful and clean. He arrived at the palace.

At the entrance, two guards signalled to him to stop. Their uniforms were tight fitting, made of fabrics the tailor had never seen, and packed with a fascinating array of weapons and communications devices.

'What is your purpose?'

The tailor explained.

'Do you have any paperwork? A purchase order from the palace?'

'No.' The tailor hesitated. 'It wasn't like that, you see –'

'Every delivery must have a signed purchase order from the appropriate department. Go away and obtain the necessary documentation.'

The tailor explained his story again. 'Please inform Prince Ibrahim that I am here. He is expecting me. My name is Mustafa the tailor. He has ordered a silk robe from me.'

'Please leave at once and do not come peddling to the king's palace.'

'Will you speak to the prince? He will remember me. . .'

But the guards would listen no more. The tailor had no option but to get back in his van and drive away.

He camped in the van and came every day to the palace to wait outside the gates. The guards proving intransigent, he scanned the windows for signs of the prince's presence, looked in every arriving car for any of the faces that had come to his shop that day, tried to imagine how he would get a message into the palace. All to no avail.

Where could he go? He owed more money than he had seen in his whole life, and it was unlikely that anyone except the prince would buy such an extravagant, outmoded robe. All he could do was to wait until someone vindicated his story.

He ate less every day in order to save his last remaining coins, and he became dirty and unkempt. By day he sat and tracked every coming and going with eyes that grew hollow with waiting. By night he had nightmares in which the prince and his band of laughing noblemen walked right by him as he lay oblivious with sleep.

The van became an expense he could not support. He drove into the desert to hide the robe, which he wrapped carefully in paper, placed in an old trunk, and buried in a spot by some trees. And he sent the vehicle back.

He became a fixture by the palace gates. The guards knew him and tolerated his presence as a deluded, but harmless, fool. Passers-by threw him coins, and some stopped to listen to his story of when the royal prince had once come to visit him and how he would one day come again. He became used to every indignity of his life happening in the full view of tourists and officials.

At night when the streets were free he wandered the skein of the city. His face shadowed by a blanket, he trudged under spasmodic streetlights, and gazed into shadowy shop windows where mannequins stood like ghosts in their urban chic. Everything seemed to be one enormous backstage, long abandoned by players and lights, where dusty costumes and angular stage sets lay scattered amid a dim and eerie silence. There danced in his head the memory of a search, a saviour, but it too was like the plot of a play whose applause had long ago become silence.

Years passed. He knew not how many.

One night, as he walked past a cheap restaurant where taxi drivers and other workers of the night sat under a fluorescent glow shot through with the black orbits of flies, he saw that there were some unaccustomed guests eating there. A crowd of men sat eating and drinking and laughing with beautiful women, all of them in clothes not from this part of town. And with a shock that roused him from years of wearied semi-consciousness, he realized that one of them was Prince Ibrahim.

'Your Highness!' cried the tailor, rushing into the restaurant and flinging himself to the floor. Everyone looked up at the bedraggled newcomer, and bodyguards immediately seized him to throw him out. But the prince interjected, looking round at his friends and laughing, 'Wait! Let us see what this fellow wants!'

Everyone fell silent and looked at the tailor as he stood in the centre of the room, fluorescent lights catching the wispy hair on the top of his head.

'Your Highness, many years ago you came to my tailor's shop in a small town far from here and ordered a silk robe with your royal insignia of the stag and crescent moon. I spent four months making the finest robe for you, but when I came to your palace no one believed my story or allowed me to make my delivery. I wrote you letters and waited for you day and night, but all to no avail. I have spent all the years since then living in the gutter and waiting for the day I would find you again. And now I appeal to your mercy: please help me.'

Everyone looked at Ibrahim. 'Is he speaking the truth?' one of the men asked.

The prince looked irately at the tailor, saying nothing. Another man spoke up.

'I was with you that day, prince. The tailor's story is true. Do you not remember?'

The prince did not look at him. Slowly he said: 'Of course I remember.'

He continued to stare at the insignificant figure in the centre of the room. 'But this is not the man. He is an impostor.

The tailor I saw that day never brought what I ordered. Get this cheat out of here.'

And the bodyguards threw the tailor into the street.

But the prince's companion, whose name was Suleiman, felt sorry for him. As the party of men and women heated up behind steamed-up windows and its separate elements began to coalesce, he sneaked out to catch up with him.

'Sir! Stop!' The tailor turned round, and Suleiman ran up to meet him.

'Allow me to present myself. My name is Suleiman, and I was present when the prince came to your shop several years ago. I feel partially responsible that you are in this situation. Tell me your story.'

Standing in the dark of the street, the tailor told him everything. Suleiman was much moved. Overhead, the night sky glistened with stars like sequins.

'Listen Mustafa, I would like to buy this robe from you myself. I know it will be an exquisite object, and I feel unhappy at the idea that you will continue to suffer as you are now. Take my car, fetch the robe, bring it to my house, and I will pay you for it.'

In the splendid steel surrounds of a black Mercedes the tailor flew along the smooth tarmac of the national highway as it cut into the rippling desert and its lanes reduced from six to four, to two. He watched the prudently designed cars of the national automobile company flash past each other in 180-degree rectitude, and, fighting off the drowsiness of the heat and the hypnotic landscape in order to concentrate on the road, he looked out for the lone group of trees under which he had deposited the trunk.

When at last the Mercedes came to rest at the spot, he was surprised to see that there was a crowd of people there. It looked as if some sort of major construction was going on. Muddy jeeps were parked around the area, and under the blinding glare of the sun a team of men painstakingly measured out the land with poles and ropes while local people stood around and watched. Terror wrung the tailor's organs as he approached one of the spectators to ask what was happening.

'You don't know? A great discovery has been made here! A poor villager found a trunk containing a magnificent silk robe right in this spot. He took it to the city where an antique specialist identified it as royal ceremonial wear from the eighteenth century. He sold it to a French museum, which paid seven million dollars! Now everyone is looking for the rest of the treasure!'

What could the tailor say? Which of these people who laboured all around him in pursuit of some ancient hoard would believe his unlikely story? All he could do was to climb slowly back into the Mercedes and return to the city.

Eventually the car returned to the leafy streets it knew well, all iron railings and columns, and the tailor found himself climbing the stone steps to the mighty front door of Suleiman's residence. He was greeted by his would-be patron's wife, who welcomed him warmly, sat him down and surrounded him with a plush arrangement of mint tea and sweetmeats. Finally Suleiman himself entered.

'You return empty-handed, tailor! How could this be?'

The tailor told him what he had found. Suleiman, looked at him with some uncertainty.

'How do I know that there ever was a robe?'

The tailor had no answer.

The three of them sat in a tense silence that was flecked only with the occasional sound of cup on saucer. Finally the tailor got up to leave. Suleiman took him aside.

'My good fellow. You do seem honest enough, but given the circumstances, I don't know if I can really help you. Here's some money for your board and food. I hope your lot improves.'

Once a year in that land there was a festival whose name roughly translates as the 'Day of Renewal'. This was an ancient custom, a day of merrymaking and of peace between all citizens. Gifts were given to children, prisoners were set free, and there were public feasts. All the royal residences were opened up to the general public, who could enjoy food and music in the gardens. Everyone was happy on that day: there was handshaking in the streets between strangers, flags fluttered gaily from every rooftop, and the sky became thick with kites. Of late, foreign corporations wishing to show their commitment to the nation had become particularly extravagant in their support for this festival. Pepsi gave out free drink in all public places, Ford selected 'a worthy poor family' to receive the gift of its latest model, and Citibank surprised its ATM customers with cash prizes given out at random throughout the day. And, in the afternoon, the king would hear the cases of those who were in need of redress.

The tailor came to the palace early, but there was already a row of aggrieved citizens waiting. As each one arrived, a kindly attendant noted down the details of the case. Then a bailiff called them, one by one. At length, it was the tailor's turn.

At the far end of the vast marble room, the king sat on a throne surmounted by a canopy of silk and jewels. Down either side sat rows of learned men. To the right of the king was Prince Ibrahim. His blue pinstriped suit contrasted elegantly with his sandstone face, on which a shapely beard was etched like the shadow of butterfly wings.

'Approach, tailor,' said the king patiently. 'Tell us your matter.'

Pairs of bespectacled eyes followed the tailor as he walked across the echoing expanse towards the throne in the new shoes he had bought for the occasion. He stood for a moment trying to collect himself. And then, once again, he told his story.

As the king listened, he became grave.

King Saïd believed that the simple goodness and wisdom of village people was the best guarantee of the future prosperity and moral standing of the country. The possibility that his own son might have taken it upon himself to tread down this small-town tailor was therefore distressing. The prince's lack of constancy was a continual source of disquiet for the king, and the tailor's narrative unfortunately possessed some degree of verisimilitude. On the other hand, he received many claims of injustice every day and most turned out, on inspection, to be false.

As the tailor finished, he spoke thus:

'This is a case of some difficulty, tailor. There is much here that it is impossible for me to verify. What say you, my son?'

'As you know, my Lord and Father, I have the greatest sympathy with the needy of our land. But his story is preposterous.'

'Is it possible that you could have failed to recall the events of which the tailor speaks?'

'Of course not.'

King Saïd pondered.

'Tailor, our decision in this case will hinge on your moral character. It will not be possible today for us to verify the details of what happened so long ago, the fate of the clothes you say you made, or your financial situation. I am therefore going to ask you to demonstrate your moral worth by telling us a story. According to our traditions.'

Utter silence descended on the room, and all watched the tailor, expectantly.

'Your Highness, I have now been in this capital city for some time. And I recently met another tailor who told me the following tale.

'There once came to his shop a wealthy man who was about to be married. This man ordered a luxurious set of wedding clothes. The tailor was honoured and overjoyed and went out to celebrate with his family.

'It so happened that the bridegroom had a lover, a married woman from the city. Each visit she made to him he vowed would be the last. But he never seemed to be able to broach the subject of their rupture before their clothes and their words had dissolved between them and they were left only with their lovemaking.

'Ignorant of this, the tailor began to order the finest fabrics for the wedding clothes. But as he set to work on the new garments, the cloth simply melted away as he cut it. Again and again he chalked out designs – but each time the same thing happened, until all of the valuable cloth had disappeared.

'When the bridegroom came to collect the clothes he was furious to discover they were not ready, and demanded an explanation.

'"I think the explanation lies with you," replied the tailor. "Since your wedding clothes refused to be made, I can only suppose you are not ready to wear them. Tell me this: what colour are the eyes of your bride-to-be?"

'The bridegroom thought hard, but the image of his lover stood resolutely between him and the eyes of his betrothed, and he was unable to answer.

'"Next time you come to me for clothes," said the tailor, "make sure you are prepared to wear them."

'With that, the young man left the tailor, called off his marriage, and left the city.'

The tale hung in the air for a while, and dispersed.

'What do you say, scholars, to the tailor's story?' asked the king.

'Sire,' replied one, 'it is a fine story, constructed according to our traditions, and possessing all the five levels of meaning prized in the greatest of our writings.'

'My son, what do you think?'

'There is no doubt that this fellow is accomplished in the realm of fantasy.'

The king looked pained.

'I myself think that the tailor has proved himself to be a man of the greatest integrity and probity. Such a man will never seek to advance himself through untruth. Tailor, I can see there has been a series of culpable misunderstandings as a result of which you have suffered greatly. Tell me what you would like from us.'

'Sire, I am sunk so low that all I can ask for is money.'

'Tailor, consider it done. We shall settle all your debts. Please go with this man, my accountant Salim. He will tell you what papers you need to provide and will give you all the necessary forms to fill in. We are heartily sorry for the difficulties you have had to encounter. Go back to your village and resume your life.'

*

Mustafa the tailor was anxious to leave the city, whose streets had by now become poisoned with his memories. But he did not wish to return to his village. It seemed too small to contain the thoughts he now had in his head.

He took up residence in a distant seaside town where he made a living sewing clothes and uniforms for sailors. In the afternoons, when his work was done, he would sit by the shore looking into the distance, and tell stories to the masts of boats that passed each other on the horizon.

Contributors

ABRAHAM VERGHESE

Abraham Verghese is the director of The Center for Medical Humanities and. Ethics at the University of Texas Health Science Center at San Antonio, and he is Marvin Forland Distinguished Professor of Medicine. A graduate of Madras University, Verghese trained as a resident and chief resident in internal medicine at East Tennessee State University, and as a fellow in infectious diseases at Boston University. He has served on the faculty at various universities, and is board certified in internal medicine, pulmonary diseases and infectious diseases.

In 1990–91, Dr Verghese attended the Iowa Writers Workshop at the University of Iowa where he obtained a Master of Fine Arts degree. His first book, *My Own Country*, about AIDS in rural Tennessee, was a finalist for the National Book Critics Circle Award for 1994 and was made into a movie. His second book, *The Tennis Partner*, was a *New York*

Times notable book and a national bestseller. He has published extensively in medical journals, and his writing has appeared in *The New Yorker*, *Sports Illustrated*, *The Atlantic Monthly*, *Esquire*, *Granta*, *The New York Times Magazine*, *The Wall Street Journal* and elsewhere.

GITHA HARIHARAN

Githa Hariharan's first novel, *The Thousand Faces of Night* (1992), won the Commonwealth Writers Prize. Since then, she has published a collection of stories, *The Art of Dying* (1993), followed by three novels, *The Ghosts of Vasu Master* (1994), *When Dreams Travel* (1999) and *In Times of Siege* (2003). She has also edited *A Southern Harvest*, a volume of stories in English translation from four major South Indian languages, and co-edited a collection of stories for Indian children, *Sorry, Best Friend!* Hariharan's work has been translated into French, Spanish, Italian, Dutch and Greek; her essays and fiction have also been included in several collections and anthologies, such as Salman Rushdie's *Mirrorwork: 50 Years of Indian Writing 1947–1997*.

The Winning Team, a collection of stories for children, was published in 2004. Also in 2004, Vintage brought out the paperback edition of *In Times of Siege*.

VIVEK NARAYANAN

Vivek Narayanan has lived in India, southern Africa and the United States. His short stories have appeared or are forthcoming in *Agni*, *Best New American Voices* (Harcourt, USA, 2004), *The Post-Post Review* (Bombay) and *Mamba* (Durban, South Africa, 1999). His poems have recently appeared in *Harvard Review*, *Fulcrum* and *Rattapallax*; and in the anthology, *Reasons for Belonging: Fourteen Contemporary Indian Poets* (Viking Penguin, 2002).

MANJULA PADMANABHAN

Manjula Padmanabhan (b.1953) is a writer and artist living in New Delhi. Her books include *Hot Death, Cold Soup* (Kali for Women, 1996), *Getting There* (Picador India, 1999), *This is Suki!* (Duckfoot Press, 2000) and *Kleptomania* (Penguin India, 2004). *Harvest,* her fifth play, won the 1997 Onassis Award for Theatre. It was published by Kali for Women in 1998 and subsequently in three separate international anthologies. She has illustrated 23 books for children including her two recent novels for children, *Mouse Attack* and *Mouse Invaders* (Macmillan Children's Books, UK, and Picador India, 2003/ 2004). Her comic strips appeared weekly in *The Sunday Observer* (Bombay, 1982–86) and daily in *The Pioneer* (New Delhi, 1991–97). Her most recent exhibition was of etchings and lithographs (London, December 2003).

NAVTEJ SARNA

Navtej Sarna is the author of the novel *We Weren't Lovers Like That* and *The Book of Nanak.* His short stories have been broadcast over the BBC World Service and have appeared in *The London Magazine* and the *Signals* and *Signals 2* anthologies (UK). He contributes book reviews to *The Times Literary Supplement, Biblio, The Little Magazine* and other journals.

A member of the Indian Foreign Service since 1980, he is presently the spokesperson for the Foreign Office in Delhi, and has earlier served as a diplomat in Moscow, Warsaw, Thimphu, Geneva, Tehran and Washington DC.

MANJU KAPUR

Manju Kapur teaches English at Miranda House College, Delhi University. Her first book, *Difficult Daughters*, won the Commonwealth Prize (Eurasia region) for best first book in 1999. Her second book, *A Married Woman*, was shortlisted for the 2004 Society of Authors' Encore Award (for best second book). Her work has been translated into numerous languages.

SHANKAR VEDANTAM

Shankar Vedantam is a national correspondent for *The Washington Post*. The winner of numerous journalism awards, Vedantam also writes fiction and plays. His short stories have been published in *Rosebud* and *Catamaran* magazines. *Tom, Dick & Harriet*, Vedantam's first play, won several playwriting awards and was produced in Philadelphia in April 2004. Vedantam's second play, *Flying While Brown*, is about civil liberties in America. The short story published here, 'The Scoop', is part of a linked collection called *The Ghosts of Kashmir* that will be published in India in 2005. Vedantam lives in Washington DC. His website is www.vedantam.com.

SAMIT BASU

Samit Basu's debut novel, *The Simoqin Prophecies* (Penguin India, 2004), was India's first genre fantasy novel in English. He is currently writing the second part of a planned trilogy. Basu was born in Calcutta, just in time to catch the last two weeks of the seventies. He graduated in economics before getting a Masters in broadcast journalism from London. He has worked for *The Telegraph* and *Outlook* magazine, and has always been a Good Bengali Boy, apart from a brief rebellious phase when he dropped out of IIM Ahmedabad to write.

ANITA RAU BADAMI

Anita Rau Badami is the author of two critically acclaimed, bestselling novels, *Tamarind Mem* and *The Hero's Walk*. Both have been published in several countries. In 2000, Anita won the Marian Engel Award for excellence in fiction for a body of work. *The Hero's Walk* won the 2001 Commonwealth Prize for the Caribbean and Canada region.

FARRUKH DHONDY

Farrukh Dhondy was born in Pune and educated there and in Cambridge, UK. He has worked in television and written several books of fiction. Today he writes films, books and occasionally works as a columnist. His latest book is *Adultery and Other Stories* and his most recent films are *The Rising*, *American Daylight* and *Take Three Girls*.

AMITAVA KUMAR

Amitava Kumar is the author of *Passport Photos* (2000), *Bombay-London-New York* (2002), and *Husband of a Fanatic* (2004). He is a professor of English at Pennsylvania State University.

SHAUNA SINGH BALDWIN

Shauna Singh Baldwin was born in Montreal and grew up in India. She is the author of *English Lessons and Other Stories* and co-author of *A Foreign Visitor's Survival Guide to America*. Shauna's awards include India's Nehru Award (gold medal),

Shastri Award (silver medal), the 1995 Writer's Union of Canada Award for short prose and the 1997 Canadian Literary Award. *English Lessons* received the 1996 Friends of American Writers Award. Her first novel, *What the Body Remembers*, received the 2000 Commonwealth Writers Prize for the Caribbean and Canada region and has been translated into eleven languages. In 2004, Knopf Canada published her second novel, *The Tiger Claw*.

Rana Dasgupta

Rana Dasgupta was born in England in 1971, and grew up in Cambridge. Having lived in France, Malaysia and the US, he moved to Delhi in 2001. 'The Tailor' is an extract from his first novel, *Tokyo Cancelled*, published by HarperCollins.